HONOR FIRST

Honor First

Harry "Buddy" Beckett

Artistic Spaces Publishing
Murfreesboro, TN

Credits:

Cover design © 2008 Jennifer Beckett

I Can't Forget You © 2006 Harry "Buddy" Beckett

Library of Congress Control Number: 2008905494

Subject Headings

    1. Historical Fiction

    2. Romance

ISBN 10: 0-9796328-3-8

ISBN 13: 978-0-9796328-3-9

Published by: Artistic Spaces Publishing Company

                    P.O. Box 330703

                    Murfreesboro, TN 37133-0703

This book is generally dedicated to all who live by their principles every day. But it is specifically dedicated to Lois Collins Rimmer for her recommendations while laboring through my manuscript and for her perception to appropriately title this book.

CONTENTS

PROLOGUE

The years between 1840 and 1860 were happy times for the Perry family living in western Virginia. But when South Carolina seceded from the Union in December 1860, uncertainty replaced peacefulness. The ebullient conversations at the general store about what the South would do in a short time, didn't much concern Johnson Lee Perry, the oldest living child of Andrew Lee and Lola Mae Perry. He was a humble and courteous young boy and quite content to do his share of work on his parents' five hundred-acre farm. The farm was situated in the broad, fertile valley north of Lewisburg, where the James River Turnpike passed through the town to the Ohio River. He was healthy and indeed happy with an abundance of everything he needed.

By March of 1861, six other Southern States seceded from the Union. Their order of withdrawal was Mississippi, Florida, Alabama, Georgia, Louisiana, and Texas. Johnson was aware of what was happening but believed the division of North and South would not affect him in sparsely settled western Virginia.

Fort Sumter, a Union possession situated in the Charleston, South Carolina harbor, was fired on by the South on April 12, 1861. The Confederate States of America was established, and in April, Virginia, Arkansas, North Carolina, and Tennessee also joined the Confederacy. Johnson was beginning to be concerned about his possible involvement in the conflict until July 1861 when Northern troops retreated in disorder after the first Battle of Bull Run (Manassas). He then believed, as did many other southern people, that there would not be much of a war. But in February 1862, the North had a victorious month with the capture of Fort Henry and Fort Donelson in Tennessee.

The Confederacy started to draft soldiers in April 1862. Healthy white males, ages eighteen to forty, were required to register. Johnson was seventeen and for the first time, knew he would see action. He stood with the Southern cause and would, of course, serve if needed. A seesaw of victories and defeats for both sides occurred during the remaining months of 1862. The Union took Memphis, Tennessee in June. The Confederate army saved Richmond on July the first in the Battle of the Seven Days. Southern troops were again victorious in the second Battle of Bull Run in late August. Confederates retreated after being defeated in September at the bloody Battle of Antietam (Sharpsburg). The Confederates dealt a crushing blow to the Union in the December Battle of Fredericksburg.

Johnson was suddenly not so ready to serve after what happened one hot day in late July of 1862. He was working in a hay field when a wagon stopped at his house. The driver briefly talked to his dad and then proceeded on his way. Johnson stopped and watched as the wagon passed by the hay field. Three young girls sat in the back of the wagon. But he only stared at one. Her hair was flaming red, and her complexion looked white as snow. She appeared to be near his age. Johnson just stood and looked at her until the wagon had passed by. When she turned to look back, he still had his blue eyes fixed on the most beautiful girl he had ever seen. The young girl with red hair was looking at a shirtless, suntanned boy with a mop of black hair. He stood six feet tall with broad, muscular shoulders and arms.

At the supper table he learned the wagon driver was Eli Foster, father of the new family who had moved to a nearby 200-acre farm last month. Mr. Foster was inquiring if he could hire a boy for a few days' work. He had three girls and no boys. The girls worked a great deal but could not do the heavy lifting required to repair the barn.

Three days later, Johnson reported for work and had lunch with the Foster family. Sitting at the same table with Sally Lou Foster made it difficult for him to swallow his food. She would serve him water while working, and by the third day, they were starting to talk. Most of their conversation was about the war and the draft.

It wasn't long, however, before Sally Lou and Johnson were often at the general store at the same time. By December, they were sitting together at church. He then, for sure, had everything he needed to be happy. Family members, church congregation, and people in the community smiled in their presence, seemingly approving that they should be together. Johnson and Sally Lou were by then greatly concerned about the fighting and their future, since he would be eighteen on Christmas Eve. They began to listen to opinions and predictions about the war with a renewed interest.

Johnson Lee Perry wiped tears as he said goodbye to family, friends, and Sally Lou. During the two weeks between Christmas and the day he left for the war, Johnson and Sally Lou were together for a few hours every day. With his leaving imminent, they became more open with their feelings and expressions, and seriously considered marriage before being separated by the war. Their discussions were of a more hopeful theme than a practical one. They assessed that the past year (1862) was not a decisive year for either side but believed the South would soon be victorious. On this judgment, they agreed to marry when he returned from the war. Of course, they couldn't know about the forthcoming Battle of Gettysburg in July, which marked a turning point in the war when the South was defeated. By the end of 1863, many believed the North would be the victor. But the stubborn Southern resistance prolonged the fighting throughout 1864 and into April 1865 when Lee surrendered to Grant at Appomattox Court House.

In front of family and friends, on a cold January day in 1863, Johnson and Sally Lou clumsily embraced (for the first time) and experienced a soul-stirring kiss. Other kisses had been "pecks."

As their fingertips parted, a sad, scared young man promised to return. His pledge and the warmth of her quivering lips were to be ever in his heart and mind. That moment in Johnson Perry's life gave him strength to overcome unimaginable hardships in the War Between the States.

CHAPTER 1

... *a glint of light* ...

Snow was suddenly blowing so hard Johnson Perry could barely move forward. He was leaning into the wind, using his last measure of energy to keep moving. About an hour earlier, the snow started and had steadily increased until he couldn't always see the road. He was walking west on the James River Turnpike on his way to Lewisburg, West Virginia. After being discharged four weeks ago, he left Richmond, Virginia and had made reasonably good time until the blowing snow started. Just over an hour ago, he was told by a farmer that the town of Clifton Forge was only a mile or so down the road.

Johnson didn't know what happened to the town, but he did know he had to have shelter soon from the cold, driving snow. After all the misery and hardships he had endured during his soldiering, thoughts of dying so close to home were circulating in his numbed mind. Troubled with his despairing thoughts, he moved forward in slow steps while hopelessness was compassing about his tired body. Only thoughts of Sally Lou were sending signals to his muscles to keep moving. "Come back to me Johnson—I am waiting for you to return," was ringing in his head. During the past two years while fighting for the South, that clarion call had, countless times, lifted him above the pain and adversities of which he would have never believed possible before entering the Army. Now he was wondering if the howling wind was vanquishing Sally Lou's unmistakable clear, sharp pledge.

Slowly walking onward, he leaned more forward to resist the strong wind. When the wind and snow suddenly stopped, he fell on his right side. While falling, a glint of light was detected before he collapsed on the road. The blinding snow returned, and there was no light. He dismissed it as a hallucination. While lying crumpled in the snow, a compelling impulse to go to sleep surged through his nearly frozen body. His reserves were all used, including mental faculties to push his body beyond seemingly impossible feats. He called her name, "Sally Lou." Again, he called her name. There was no answer and no impetus to get up. The dark night seemed to swallow up his resolve to charge onward. A faint thought, "I'm almost home" crept through his freezing mind before he went to sleep.

He couldn't discern how long he had been asleep when his eyes opened. In a dizzy stupor, he looked around to appraise his situation. It seemed minutes before a sense of comprehension overpowered his weariness to realize what was happening. Actually, nothing was happening. The wind had stopped—only flurries silently floated to the white ground. Eerie quietness filled the cold air. The reprieve from bucking the wind restored enough energy for Johnson to rise. He saw the light again. During his soldiering days, each battle he had survived was an investment in a surprising compounded power of endurance. Even with so many withdraws lately, he arose and started walking the fifty yards toward the dim light.

The wind and snow pelted him with renewed fury halfway to his last bit of hope of seeing Sally Lou again—but he knew the cabin was attainable. Smoke was coming out of the chimney, and the sight of the light in the window was more welcome than the stretcher-bearers had been on the battlefield. Before seeing the light, he was at the limit of his endurance. During the war, he had experienced intense pain and hardship, and he couldn't understand why it seemed his life was now ending. Another thing he couldn't understand was why the blinding snow stopped so he could clearly see the cabin light. This mystery would cause him hours of concern later.

Holding a post, Johnson pulled his half-frozen body onto the cabin porch. Without hesitation, he tapped on the front door and waited for an acknowledgement. None came. Inside, Carrie Butler quietly snatched the rifle from behind her bed. He repeated his tapping—but louder. He shivered and waited. Just before a third try, he heard a strong demanding voice.

"What do you want?"

Johnson was surprised that the voice belonged to a woman. He answered, "Would you please help me?"

"Who are you?"

"I'm Johnson Perry. I'm discharged from the Confederate Army. I'm on my way home. I need some help please. I won't harm you." His mind could only think in short sentences and his voice was getting weaker.

With curtness dripping with disbelief, Carrie responded. "Why should I believe you? There are many bad things happening nowadays."

Just above a raspy whisper, he replied, "Open the door Ma'am and you will see that I can't harm you." He paused and then continued, "If I *could*, I wouldn't harm you. I just need a little help to get home to marry Sally Lou. I just need a little food and a little time by your fire."

Carrie Butler had been living without a man for two years. During that time, she had become fearlessly independent and protective of her daughter who came fifteen months ago. She had recently encountered some dangers as life threatening as any soldier would face on a battlefield and had learned to be cautious, cunning, and aggressive. She had survived many hardships without defeat. And now, at 9 p.m. on this Saturday night March 25, 1865, another survival decision was required. Her callused side was saying, "No," while her soft side was whispering, "Yes it will be okay—let him come in—it's cold outside." With her mellowness tucked behind her resolute boldness, Carrie positioned herself to the left side of the door and barked a command.

"Okay Mister! Remove all your weapons and throw them in the yard."

"Yes ma'am, I only have a knife and a bayonet."

"Throw them Mister!"

Mister Johnson Perry had not formed an opinion about the woman in the cabin before now. But at this moment, he catalogued her with a certain sergeant. This five-foot-two inch barking sergeant, who weighed no more than a hundred pounds, was not finished.

"Listen Mister. I have a rifle leveled on you and know how to use it. And let me tell you Mister, you will not harm me or my baby because you won't get a chance."

Carrie stopped to catch a breath. She was not shaking. She knew what she could and would do to protect herself and Jane. Using the rifle barrel, she lifted the door latch. The door swung inward. The "thing" she saw silhouetted against the snow was almost more than her eyes and heart could absorb. Standing in the doorway, slumped forward, was what she presumed to be a man. She was momentarily stunned but quickly recovered to look at what was illuminated by the coal-oil lamp.

She saw a frosted black beard on a sallow face that had flushed many times in the fervor of a Rebel charge. A fringe of unkempt black hair was visible beneath a wet, weather-beaten, wool slouch hat. The soft brim was limp upon his shoulders, except in the front where it was folded back to the elongated, crumpled crown. Stolid eyes, filled with melancholy, were looking beyond Carrie's stare as if ashamed of his appearance and his present imploring station in life. His frame looked to be tough and sinewy but was carelessly erect. The shapeliness of his form, encumbered with life providing necessities, didn't reveal latent energy that emerged as lion-like strength when aroused.

A ragged, gray jacket splattered with blue patches, with sleeves too short and not reaching to his hips, was over a soiled, butternut colored shirt. His baggy pants were either blue or gray—it was hard to tell from the kaleidoscope of various shades of blue and gray patches. A bayonet scabbard, which dangled to the left, was attached on a leather belt around his waist. His cotton, butternut shirt was bloused between his jacket and pants. Across his front, from left shoulder to right hip, was a rolled, threadbare blanket. The ends were tied to retain his only extra article of clothing—a shirt. From his right shoulder, a cloth strap and a leather strap crossed the blanket roll. The cloth strap supported a greasy haversack made from bed ticking. The leather strap held a flannel-covered canteen he had taken from a dead Yankee. Attached to the haversack was a tin cup and camping utensils. Carrie would later see a frying pan hanging over his back.

When first seeing him, her eyes couldn't linger on his shoes—really only one shoe. His right leg was a "peg leg." His foot, and half of his lower leg, had been amputated. He had fashioned a prosthesis from a tree limb by securing it to his upper leg with two leather straps. A branch limb formed a "Y" where his knee rested in the padded crotch. His remaining leg extended backward. A well-worn shoe was on his left foot. His left pant leg was tied at the ankle revealing a dirty sock that disappeared into his contorted shoe.

Standing in shreds and patches, Johnson Perry was recently a marvelous example of the model citizen soldier of the nineteenth century—the most independent soldier who had ever belonged to an organized army. But he respected authority and submissively submitted to it. When he had two complete legs, his patched pants and faded patched gray jacket, flecked with blood, became glorified by his valor, thus making them more splendid than the mail of a King Arthur knight. In a halo of fire and smoke, with death all about, he had made perilous charges and breached the enemy lines. He went to battle half clad, half armed, and most often, half fed. As a Confederate soldier, he was fighting against an enemy with unending resources, while many of the South's necessities of war were dwindling or were depleted. The "thing" standing before Carrie fought in affliction and danger, and by his courage and sense of responsibility, could claim to be as honorable as any general on either side.

The captain who discharged him knew the end was near for the South. For Johnson, his flag was furled early and his weapon grounded. The cause, for which he struggled and exposed his life's blood, was lost. But in his heart, he knew he was part of an army purified by a proud and gallant record, not equaled by any other army on earth. He could claim a victory for being a Johnny Reb.

Right now, this once screaming, charging soldier, stood mute. He was a beggar waiting for a morsel of food—waiting for Carrie to speak.

A compassionate part of her heart wanted to put down the gun, but she realigned her priorities before saying, "Come in." Then added in a firm lower tone, "Slowly, and shut the door behind you."

CHAPTER 2

. . . the last words he heard before . . .

Carrie's cabin was small but adequate to raise a family in the 1860's. Major household furniture on the main level consisted of one bed, a cook stove, a table with four chairs, and two rocking chairs. A fourteen-inch-wide poplar board, five feet long with three shelves below, was attached to the wall near the stove. The fireplace was in the end of the cabin, to the right of the front door. The kitchen was left of the door. Her bed was in the back corner from the kitchen. Two sleeping mats were in a loft accessible by a ladder.

Johnson was standing in front of the fireplace, trying to comprehend his circumstances, when he heard
another command from Carrie.

"Mister! Don't move while I fix you some food. I will
tell you again that this rifle is ready to fire. If you try
anything I consider a threat to me or my baby, you will
be a dead soldier that won't make it home alive."

Johnson didn't answer. He had no intentions to
harm anyone. He just wanted some food and to get
warm and be on his way. Staying in this cabin tonight
was not an option.

Carrie had directed Johnson to put some wood in
the fireplace while she was restarting the fire in the cook
stove. She had soup and four biscuits to warm. While
they were warming, she picked up her rifle and walked
to a back door. Attached to the back of the cabin was
an eight-by-eight pantry room. In the winter months,
it was a good place to keep food cool. A stone cellar
was located ten feet back of the pantry room, where all
crocks of milk and preserved food in mason jars were
kept winter and summer.

Carrie quickly returned to the kitchen with a quart
of buttermilk and placed it on the kitchen table. She then
put two pieces of cold cornbread on the table. Standing
near the cook stove with the rifle beside her, she told
her visitor to come and eat. In quickened steps, Johnson
moved to the table—the opposite end from where Carrie

was standing. He used all of his willpower to slowly eat the cornbread and drink half of the buttermilk. When the soup and biscuits were warm, she used the rifle barrel to push them half way down the table.

Less than an hour later, Johnson was asleep on the floor in the back corner by the fireplace. During his meal, he had repeatedly thanked her for her hospitality and told her he would leave after eating the best meal since leaving home. During his choppy words, he credited her several times with saving his life. Carrie sat at the opposite end of the table and slowly realized this soldier was not like two Yankees she had recently encountered. Not even like Oliver Cochran, who tried to kiss her when he visited while on furlough. Nevertheless, she would not let down her guard. "Now you listen Mister, you can sleep here, but I will watch you all night. I am young and strong and can stay awake and still do my day's work tomorrow. From what I'm hearing, we have lost the war, but since you fought for our cause, you can sleep here tonight."

These were the last words he heard before crashing into a sleep of oblivion.

The rooster crowed on schedule. Johnson was still asleep. Jane was asleep and so was Carrie. She sat at the table the night before for over an hour thinking about how the war had changed her life.

In 1860 when she was fourteen, her parents moved from Wytheville to Clifton Forge after her dad's uncle willed the farm to him. She met Earl Butler in the summer of 1861, and they were seeing each other regularly until he was drafted in June of 1862. The following January, her parents died from pneumonia. Earl came home on furlough in February of 1863 and asked to marry her. He had just been through the battle of Fredericksburg in December, where the South dealt a crushing defeat to the Union forces. He convinced her to marry him because the war couldn't last much longer, and he would be home soon to work the farm.

There were some significant facts about the resources of the North and South that Earl didn't know. The North had more than double the South's population. There were four times more bank deposits in the North than the South. The North had two and a half times more railroad mileage. And most importantly, the North had well over five times more factories.

She remembered how heartsick and lost she was from just losing her parents and how depressed about being alone. He told her he would be back for spring plowing. They married in February, and Jane was born the following November. Earl left his bride, never to see her again. He was killed in July of 1863 in the battle of Gettysburg.

When Earl left in February, and didn't return in April, she started the garden. Since her parents died, she had done all of the required work on the forty-acre farm. Her only source of income was selling and trading butter, eggs, and garden produce at the general store. She was a fully developed young lady when married at sixteen, had always worked hard, and had always been strong and healthy.

Looking ahead to another growing season was causing her to think more about Oliver Cochran. His dad, who owned the general store, said last week he was expecting him home soon based on his last letter. She didn't really like him, but with so many boys not returning from the war, she believed she didn't have a choice. Lately, long evenings alone were becoming more difficult to endure. But then she thought about being so determinedly independent these past two years—maybe she couldn't tolerate a man in her life. She and Earl only lived together six days.

After her thinking period, she had decided to recline on her bed for a short time. Below her threshold of consciousness, a subliminal perception about the stranger's character was trekking in and out of her mind. He seemed to be what he said he was—a discharged soldier going home to marry his Sally Lou. She hadn't survived for two years by acting on unproven assumptions, so the rifle was on the bed beside her. But there must have been some degree of assurance in her mind that he would not harm her and Jane, because she did finally go to sleep.

When she awoke, she was momentarily befuddled as to why she was in bed fully clothed. She then suddenly realized she had a prisoner in the cabin. Sheepishly, she restated her thoughts about the stranger, whom she noted was still asleep.

CHAPTER 3

. . . a little brittle and breakable . . .

Carrie quickly jumped out of bed and walked to the cook stove. After it was starting to heat, she put several pieces of wood in the fireplace while observing her overnight guest for any sudden movement. It was then back to the kitchen. She had plenty of work to do every day, such as: taking care of Jane, milking two times, getting milk ready to churn and make butter, taking care of the chickens and hog, cooking, washing clothes and diapers, mending the fence, cabin maintenance, splitting wood and keeping the fires going, gardening and canning food, sewing and mending, and many other things. That day, more work would be required to care for her ward.

She normally started the coffee and breakfast and then milked the cows before Jane awoke. She was a good baby with a predictable sleeping schedule, but this morning it would be breakfast first and then milking with Jane by her side. No way could Jane be alone with the stranger, even if he was asleep.

During Carrie's thinking or dreaming last night, she had decided to give the soldier some of Earl's clothes. But she first had more work to do before he awoke. Biscuits were soon ready for the oven. When the coffee and bacon were done, she called, "Mr. Johnson! Are you hungry?

Johnson was awake but was too content to move. The perfume of frying bacon and brewing coffee was permeating his mind and he thought his mamma had just called.

"Hey Mister! If you want to eat—get up now!"

The "get up now" was as clearly understood as an army order. Carrie was beginning to soften some in her heart but would not relinquish her commanding position. The inflection in her voice was still unmistakably controlling, and she still had the rifle near. She thought again how she had recently defended herself and would do it again in a heartbeat if required.

Johnson sat down at the table. Carrie was busy at the stove and didn't directly look at him as she asked, "How do you like your eggs?"

"Ma'am, any way will be fine."

"Okay, you'll get them the way I like them—sunny side up."

She didn't ask how many. He got four and two for her. Johnson thanked her again and again for the delicious food. He especially liked the fresh butter. He told her it was better than his mother's butter. While Carrie listened to accolades, she ate and fed Jane. It felt strange eating with a man, especially with a rifle in her lap. A few times she tried to visualize Earl sitting across the table from her. But this Johnson man was so dirty she could hardly look at him. She had a plan to remedy that.

He looked much older than nineteen, so she considered him a mister. "Mr. Johnson, I have some clean clothes for you. They belonged to my husband who was killed at Gettysburg. But first you have to take a bath. I'm going to do the milking, and while I'm gone you can bathe. There are two pans of water on the stove. I expect you will need one pan to scrub and the other to wash."

Carrie pointed to a chair at the table saying that clean clothes were in the seat. She then arose and bundled Jane and said in a firm but less assertive manner, "You have thirty, maybe thirty-five, minutes before I'm back. Put your old clothes on the porch."

What she saw when she returned to the cabin was as shocking as the "thing" she had seen last night. Johnson Perry was a handsome, clean-shaven young man. Last night, he didn't realize the razor in his haversack could be considered a weapon. He was sitting at the kitchen table folding the razor when Carrie entered the cabin. When he stood, she noted that the clothes fit, except the pant leg was a bit short. Carrie was so disoriented when she saw him she left the rifle on the porch, and it didn't register that he had a razor. She managed to get to the table with a pail of milk. The other pail was at the barn since she had Jane to carry. Johnson quickly informed her that he would fetch the other pail. While he was gone, she stood in the kitchen in a daze and thought how handsome he was. He also seemed to be an honorable person. She still didn't think about the razor or rifle.

She strained the milk into four large crocks and then placed them in the cool pantry. He stood at the fire-place watching her. Last night, he was so cold, hungry, and humiliated that he only dimly saw a person who barked threats. One who was a stern and authoritarian Good Samaritan. This morning after food, rest, and a clean body, his clear eyes were seeing a beautiful girl—a different kind of beauty from Sally Lou, but also pleas-ingly addictive. Her countenance was solemn but with a softness. Her static expression reflected her earnest and intense personality. Johnson would later be enraptured by her explosive smile. He noticed her quick hand move-ments and her confident bearing as she walked. Her blue calico dress, with little white flowers, was tight around her small waist, revealing noticeable hips and breasts.

He hadn't been close to this much beauty for a long time. Light brown hair was pinned up, with a few loose strands fluttering as she moved about. Her face had strong jaws with a rounded chin. Her complexion was smooth and creamy with a little blush on her cheeks. He thought her pretty face was perfectly shaped to compliment her petite body. But her most beautiful and intriguing feature was her dark brown eyes—so dark they shined as polished coal. The few times he had looked straight into them, he was mesmerized in waves of dizziness.

As soon as Carrie returned from the pantry, Johnson announced he was going to split some wood. He wasn't trying to take charge but wanted to help with some work before leaving. The first sergeant didn't object. She had mellowed considerably in the last few minutes. When Johnson went out the door, he immediately reopened it and placed the rifle inside.

Two hours later, Carrie softly called for Johnson to come in for hot coffee. He noticed the gun was still by the door when he came in. She had made some molasses cookies to have with the coffee. They both sat at the table looking at each other with an altered perception. She saw a kind, considerate man who needed some help and apparently had never harmed anyone. He saw a young girl who knew how to protect herself in a dangerous situation. But when a threat seemed to be expunged, she possessed the wisdom to civilly reevaluate.

"What's your first name Mr. Johnson?"

"Johnson."

Carrie looked confused.

"Johnson Lee Perry."

"Oh, I'm sorry."

"That's okay. What's your name?"

"Carrie. Carrie Ann Butler."

"Let me say, Carrie Ann, that's a beautiful name, and your cookies are beautiful good. But then every thing you have cooked has been the best. I will never forget your cooking."

Spinning from her thoughts, she asked, "Are you leaving today?"

"I wanted to talk about that. I don't want to be a burden . . . but . . . the . . . the . . . If I stayed one more day, I could dig a new pit and move the outhouse."

Sighing, "I know. I didn't know how I was going to get that done. It would really help me if you—"

Johnson interrupted, "Oh that's the least I can do for you after all you've done for me."

They looked at each for a long second. Johnson still got a little brittle and breakable when looking into her dark eyes under their heavy arched brows. But each time his mind walked down his stare, he lingered a little longer, gulping draughts of her natural beauty.

Carrie was finding a new, likeable feature each time she looked at him. Right now, it was how his hairline framed his face. A minute ago, it was his clear blue eyes that had looked gray last night.

As a defense to halt unfamiliar feelings from consuming him, Johnson started talking about Sally Lou. He told Carrie about some of the times she had been the inspiration he believed saved his life. Carrie maintained eye contact as much as he would permit during his narrative. Her lips seemed rosier, and her demeanor was different from last night and earlier this morning. There was calmness in her expression. This attribute, coupled with her enchanting eyes, was giving Johnson trouble with concentrating on his remarks. Last night, her pretty face was distorted with an inflexibility that conveyed her protective intentions. Now, she was so pleasing to look at that he had to move.

"Thanks for coffee and cookies. I'll split a little more wood and get started on the pit."

In a sweet lyrical statement, she replied, "I'll have lunch ready in an hour."

Carrie scolded herself for her thoughts about Johnson. She now believed he really was on his way home to marry Sally Lou. That was one of the first things he announced the night before. He was the only decent man she had seen in two years. Being alone, she knew she was right to be skeptical of him. But now, he appeared to be an all right man. She said to herself, "Come on lonely girl, not so fast. He's not the last man around here."

That made her think of Oliver Cochran, who would soon be calling. She finally decided her life wasn't turning out the way she had dreamed when she was a little girl. In her daydreaming times, her hero man actually looked and acted a lot like Johnson. He had brown eyes, but Johnson's blue ones would do.

Johnson was doing a lot of thinking also—mostly about Sally Lou. He went over and over the many times her memory had given him the needed ounce of energy to crawl another foot. Her image before him was so vivid each time he charged into a firestorm of hot lead. He remembered cold nights when he could imagine the warmth of her arms around him. His life was centered on returning to her. Since their meeting, nothing else had mattered beyond spending the rest of his life with her. No other person had been in his thoughts until this morning.

The temperature was near forty and a good day to work outside. He was feeling normal again and had split a heap of wood. He worked fast, trying to concentrate on the splitting and not on guilty feelings for thinking about Carrie. In his heart he knew he would continue home to marry Sally Lou. But first, he would help Carrie with some work she couldn't do.

When he entered the cabin for lunch, the rifle was not by the door. He later saw it by the bed. In Carrie's presence, he once again felt out of control. He didn't look at her much while they ate. She had used her canned food to fix green beans and corn. With the remaining biscuits and butter and buttermilk and cookies, another delicious meal was before Johnson.

Last night, she put some of her dried beans in water to soak, and this morning, she started slow cooking them. For supper, she would fix fried potatoes with the beans and make skillet fried cornbread cakes. She would open a jar of relish (chow chow) and slice a big onion. She would also make a raisin pie.

For two years she had cooked for herself without much imagination—often eating the same food for days. But with someone so appreciative to share the meal, she was inspired to do a little planning.

CHAPTER 4

. . . *first battle was in May of 1863*

Johnson milked Polly and Glory, fed the hog and chickens, gathered the eggs, cleaned the fireplace, and carried in wood and water before supper. This was work Carrie didn't have to do. He was happy to help her since she had been so good to him—even saved his life. She could have refused to open the door or could have shot him. A less levelheaded woman probably would have shot him.

He apologized for eating so much. Carrie knew he meant every compliment, and she was feeling better than any other time in two years. The meal was slow with a dreamy glow from the coal-oil lamp and the flickering fireplace. She had never felt this way during a meal. A shroud of contentment had settled over the table— actually in the room. All of her cautious thoughts and behavior were replaced with an attraction for Johnson she could not fling from her conscience. For the first time since being alone, a vulnerable feeling was creeping through her veins. Until now, she had defended herself against physical danger, where most women would have fainted or perished. But this new feeling seemed stronger than her will to resist. In one day, her defenses had crumbled, and she was now ready to invite this stranger into her heart and life. But what he told her about Sally Lou at lunch prevented her from humiliating both of them.

After Johnson declared he couldn't eat a third piece of pie, Carrie asked him if he would like to hold Jane while she did the dishes. He agreed and realized another page had been turned. She was accepting him into her life, free of fear or doubt—this frightened him. The way she looked at him spoke volumes to his heart. He was leaving tomorrow before noon—for sure. Each time he looked at Carrie, he believed he could be lured into writing a new chapter in his life. But Sally Lou meant too much to him to let this pretty girl lead him away from the one who had provided him with the determination to survive inconceivable hardships and return to her arms.

When Carrie took Jane, Johnson announced he was going outside. Maybe the cool March air would quench the fire smoldering within him. That was his thought as he stepped through the doorway. Pacing around the yard and thinking about Sally Lou didn't really solve anything. He started concentrating on finishing the outhouse. By ten o'clock tomorrow morning, it would be over the new pit and then he could fix the chicken house door. By eleven, he would be on his way. Then he remembered the section of fence that couldn't wait much longer before being repaired. So he guessed he would leave after that job. His thoughts wandered aimlessly a while longer before returning to the cabin.

Carrie was sitting in a rocking chair by the fireplace with Jane in her arms. She motioned for him to sit in the other rocker. Since he entered this cabin last night, he had obeyed all of her commands; he was going to obey again. But it was different now. He couldn't explain to his mind exactly what he meant—but in his heart, he knew.

He sat down before realizing she was nursing Jane. Up he jumped.

"It's okay, I'm covered."

Johnson had never been that close to a mother nursing her baby.

"Come on sit down. I'll be through shortly. About a month ago she stopped nursing, but I've been trying every day anyway. I guess it's a mother thing."

He didn't sit down, instead, he stood near the kitchen table until Carrie got up and handed him Jane without saying a word. She was putting a blanket on a clothes-line near her bed when she said in a soft commanding voice, "Johnson, I'm putting this blanket up so we can have privacy when we bathe tonight."

He squinted his eyes—remembering he bathed this morning.

"Could we talk awhile? For two years, this time of day has been so lonely for me. When my parents were living, we spent some happy times around the fireplace after supper. We sat on the porch during warm weather. I love the sound of a gentle summer rain on the metal roof."

She stopped talking and stared at the fire. After a few heartbeats, she turned to Johnson. "Would you . . . would you tell me a . . . a . . . about your leg?"

When he sat in a chair, he would loosen the lower strap around his upper leg to move his knee from the support pad. His amputated leg would dangle and be parallel to the stick peg. With most of his weight on his left leg, he could maneuver the one or two steps required to sit. His peg would then be at an angle with the floor while his right leg would be in a similar position with his left leg.

For nearly an hour, Johnson told her about his Army time. He didn't know why, but he started from the beginning when he was drafted. His first battle was in May of 1863 at Chancellorsville. The South was outnumbered but defeated the Union. Stonewall Jackson was killed. Johnson was wounded in the left arm, and while recovering contracted mumps that almost killed him. In November, while fighting at Chattanooga, Tennessee, he escaped injury but became ill with pneumonia. There was no room in the hospital, but a kind, country family agreed for him to convalesce in their home.

He told about several skirmishes that resulted in minor wounds. But in one, a wound in his side just missed vital organs. After fully mending, he barely escaped death from typhoid. But he recovered and was able to return to Virginia in April of 1864 and fight at Cold Harbor in June. Johnson seemed eager to talk about this battle, saying he almost lost his mind thinking about what happened but credited Sally Lou for him retaining his sanity. There were periods when he stared at the fireplace, as if waiting for the "forget curtain" in his mind to open and reveal events of the battle.

After Sheridan's cavalry took possession of the vital crossroads of Old Cold Harbor on Tuesday May 31, he stopped a Confederate attack, led by Lee, using newly issued repeating carbines. Johnson arrived on Wednesday with the reinforcements from the Totopotomoy Creek lines. By Thursday, the second day of June, the main armies of both sides were assembled along a seven mile line from Bethesda Church to the Chickahominy River. At dawn, Friday the third, Union forces assaulted along the Bethesda-Cold Harbor line and were slaughtered in unbelievable numbers. When Johnson mentioned slaughter, he gazed at the curling flames a long time before continuing.

When he spoke again, his voice was low and rippled with sadness. He was told that over 12,000 yanks were lost while the South lost something over 2,000. He said to Carrie that at times he would stop shooting and vomit. His sergeant bellowed at him to keep shooting. It was so awful, so senselessly unnecessary for General Grant to keep attacking when the Confederates had battlefield advantage and the yanks fell like cutting hay. There were times he didn't care if he fell, but he didn't get a scratch. (Recorded history states 6,000 Union soldiers were killed in a one hour period. It is also recorded that General Grant said this was one attack he wished he had never ordered.)

Johnson was later stationed at Richmond, and while on patrol one night, he was shot in the ankle. It happened two days before Christmas of 1864. He was hit with the dreadful conical minne ball that weighed over an ounce. It was fired from a rifled musket with a higher velocity than from the smoothbore guns. When the minne ball hit his ankle bones, they were shattered to total destruction. The lower velocity smoothbore ball fractured a bone that could often be restored with a splint. There was but one treatment for him. By 1864, surgeons had learned to amputate considerably above the affected area. Johnson, even so, considered himself lucky that he had half of his lower leg left.

He told Carrie about the hospital where his leg was amputated. She seemed to enjoy hearing about things and places she had never seen. Johnson methodically described the hospital, starting with how the wounded men were transported to the hospital. She cringed when explained the transport wagons had no springs, and some soldiers died from the bumpy ride en route to the hospitals. Most wounds were treated within forty-eight hours at field hospital tents near the front line.

He told her about the awful conditions in the surgeon's tent. The surgeon and his assistants were shirtless and bespattered with blood as they stood at a chest-high table holding down screaming victims. The patients (victims) would scream and holler when told they were going to lose a limb or limbs. The cries usually didn't stop until chloroform (when available) was administered. Johnson heard many mournful pleas from operations before his turn on the chest-high table. Carrie cried when she heard him say the surgeons amputated fast and then threw the severed limb on a nearby pile of mangled limbs.

His convalescing hospital was better than the field tents. It was a two-story building once used to manufacture carriages and wagons. An incline ramp connected the two floors. The upper floor was covered with clean wheat straw about a foot deep. Johnson was assigned a space on the straw. The more severely wounded were placed in rough lumber bunks on the first floor.

Listening to Johnson vaulted Carrie to an emotional high never before experienced. Her life had been more repetitious than exciting. She had learned simple ways to survive and had never been exposed to thrilling and stimulating adventures. She knew Johnson faced death many times, but he had seen and done things she couldn't even imagine. Her young days were spent happily roaming the woods and creeks because there were no other opportunities to stimulate the mind of a little girl.

Carrie intently listened. She had waited forever, it seemed, to sit by the fire and have a conversation. She didn't talk much, but just to be with another person in the evening had her spirits soaring. She was intoxicated with a feeling of contentment that was laced with serenity. But in her life she had not let dreaming or idle thoughts dominate much of her time. She was a person of schedules and action. She had to be that way to survive living alone. Johnson had grown quiet while looking at bouncing flames. He too was enjoying a measure of contentment before Carrie interrupted his reverie.

"I'll fix our bath water. Do you have a chew stick (a thin twig with a frayed end used as a toothbrush)?"

"Yes."

He tightened his lips while thinking, "I had a bath this morning." There had been times he didn't bathe for days and days—even weeks.

CHAPTER 5

The fire whisked their thoughts up the chimney . . .

The one-room cabin was partially sprayed with a blue sheen from a full moon. The fire was flickering, and Carrie was warm and cozy and feeling protected with a trustful man in the cabin. Behind the hanging blanket by her bed, she bathed and put on her nightgown. Johnson bathed at the kitchen stove and went to sleep on his floor pallet by the fireplace. Talking about the Cold Harbor battle relieved his mind from some of the torment and anguish that had been affecting his sleep. Tonight, he had quickly drifted into a deep peacefulness. A few feet from him, in the other back corner of the cabin, Carrie lay wide-awake.

The quintessence that filled her being while sitting by the fire had changed to a tempest within her. She was alternating between sadness and happiness. Gusts of sorrow were blowing from her time with Earl. On her wedding day, she was terrified about what was supposed to happen. And it didn't take long for *it* to happen. They were married before noon and were in bed at 2 p.m. He took full advantage of his six-day honeymoon before returning to his Army unit.

Waves of happiness skipped within her when Johnson rolled into her mind. He didn't linger long before Sally Lou came on the scene, and her blissfulness ebbed to sorrow. These yin and yang feelings, coupled with her honeymoon pity party, were jerking her mind into spasms of sleeplessness. But she finally went to sleep.

After what seemed like a short time, she was suddenly awake and bolted up in bed. She hurriedly, but quietly, walked to Johnson and whispered, "Johnson, there's somebody outside."

He didn't awake. She bent over and took his hand.

"Wha . . . Oh Sally Lou. Sally Lou you're here."

"Shh . . . it's Carrie—somebody's out back!"

Johnson blinked, trying to focus his eyes and mind.

At that precise moment, he dreamed it was the day he left for the army, and Sally Lou was holding his hand. Carrie only had on her gown, and as she was leaning down close to him, the loose top was drooping. Most of her breasts were exposed. She didn't know this as she was whispering her urgent message.

"What!"

"Shh . . . somebody's out back."

He blinked again, rolled to his side to change his view, and whispered.

"Do you have another gun?"

"Yes."

"Okay. You go to the loft. I'll hand Jane up to you."

She ran to her bed and put on her apron. In the pocket was her derringer pistol. Since Earl left, she had always worn her apron with the small gun in the pocket.

Johnson strapped his peg leg over his long underwear and went out the front door. The night was clear and bright. After not seeing any movement at the barn, he went to the back corner of the cabin, stopped, and then moved as fast as he could to the cellar. With his back to the stone front, he noticed the pantry room door hinges had been crudely ripped off. Twenty feet from the door, he challenged a noise inside.

"Throw out your gun and come out with your hands up!"

The noise stopped.

"Come out now!"

Carrie could hear his loud demands.

It all happened so quickly. Johnson Perry didn't survive months of fighting by spending a lot of time deciding when or if to shoot—he reacted instantly. The lead ball hit an inch over the right eye. When Carrie heard the shot, she knew she could take out one and maybe two intruders if Johnson was dead. Not knowing if he were dead or alive, she was more scared than any other time in her eighteen years. Had she been alone, all responsibility to protect Jane would have been hers. But with a man in the house, she passed the obligation to him and was relegated to the loft. Now, if her protector were dead, she would be Jane's buttress. Last night when Johnson revived from exhaustion, she concluded he could have molested or killed her, but she had remained calm. Tonight, however, she passed the torch to Johnson and was presently shaking from fear. It seemed forever before she heard his peg leg thump on the front porch.

When he entered the cabin after the excitement out back, he quickly told Carrie (after a smile) about the black bear he shot. Then he noticed she was crying. She had been so afraid for Johnson's safety that she was pale from not breathing.

Tears actually spewed out when she heard his "thump" on the front porch. Hearing him overwhelmed her stable senses and the flood of tears cascaded down her embarrassed face. "What's happening? Why am I crying?" buzzed in her dizzy head. A little over twenty-four hours ago, She had the rifle and was giving orders. Now tonight, one short day later, he had the gun and had ordered her to the loft. So abruptly, her distrust and uncertainty about him had changed to esteem and certitude. Beyond those feelings, she wouldn't let her heart have full rein and admit to herself that an embryo of amorous affection was also developing. It took her a couple minutes before she could leave the loft.

For Carrie, the black bear drama had so stimulated her emotions that an enchanted blissfulness filled her heart. She was enthralled with happiness like never before, and was so proud of Johnson for bravely going outside to investigate and protect her and Jane.

The fire slowly warmed Johnson's foot. He had rushed out without his shoe. But it wasn't all that bad. More than once, he had been without shoes before his amputation. Many Confederate soldiers marched and fought on the battlefield without shoes even during winter months.

Both could feel something happening. They were in the rocking chairs and had not spoken for minutes. She was still in her gown and apron, and he was still in his long underwear. Starting with the noise out back and the nervous expectation after the gunshot, the last several minutes had been so intense that Carrie just then became aware of the way they were dressed. She gathered the top of her gown in her hand and walked to the bed, returning with one of Earl's shirts over her shoulders.

In warm words Carrie asked a question, "Johnson, what's going to happen to the bear?"

He didn't answer. His mind was wondering what Sally Lou was doing.

"Johnson?"

"Oh! Yes! I'm going to butcher it in the morning. I mean when it's daylight."

"Did you think an intruder was in the pantry? The reason I ask is because last month two Yankees broke in the cellar."

"Yes, but you didn't need to worry. I would have shot him just like the bear."

Johnson was staring at the fire while talking and didn't move his eyes until a long second after his last word. Suddenly, he turned her way and half-shouted, "What! Yankees in the cellar? What happened?"

Carrie didn't answer. She just looked at the fire.

"Carrie, did they harm you? Well, did they?"

Johnson was controlling the conversation and spoke in authority demanding an answer. Carrie seemingly was subordinated. Finally, barely audible, "No."

"What happened—tell me. Did they get anything?"

Still, in soft low words, she spoke as she turned in his

direction. "I may tell you later. I'm going to bed now—think you can sleep?"

There was no answer. Carrie didn't get up—neither did he. The fire whisked their thoughts up the chimney for another few seconds before Johnson announced he was going to bed. He said it in a tone indicating he didn't hear her question. He did hear her but had been essentially immobile because her closeness was drawing energy from his body and mind. He was remembering what he saw when she was leaning over him and telling about the noise out back. He had never seen bared breasts before. He had never been in a situation like that. And now, they both were scantly dressed sitting four feet apart—just the two of them—oh, he wished it was morning.

To their mutual surprise, both were soon asleep. Johnson knew he had to leave tomorrow. He would take care of the bear and fix the fence and leave right after lunch. For Sally Lou's sake, he had to leave. Somehow, he turned his thoughts to a happy life with her, and on waves of gratefulness for having Sally Lou, he let reflections of this most exciting day melt away.

Carrie looked at the ceiling for awhile without lingering on any particular theme. Her mind was summarizing the events since Johnson knocked on the door. She didn't try to analyze her feelings for Johnson, nor did she try to predict the future. For the present, she felt safe with him in the cabin. A peaceful contentment fluttered through her veins as her mind slowly let go of this most exciting day.

CHAPTER 6

. . . the anticipation was unfamiliar . . .

Johnson's second full day (Monday) with Carrie began with hearing a rooster crow. He then heard clanging and banging as she placed wood in the stove. When his eyes got focused, he saw a most remarkable picture. In dim light, Carrie was busy starting breakfast. Two times, she lifted a stove cap, and the yellow flames lit her face. The firelight glow spotlighted her plain lucid beauty, which disturbed him more than he expected. This picture would later replay many times in his memory.

Last night, he believed they began to cross a bridge. A bridge leading to a place he shouldn't go. In her presence, a happiness warmed him like he had never experienced before. But it was different than his joyous association with Sally Lou. This happiness was wrapped in pain and anguish that had him cowering in shame. In the dim light of the cozy cabin, he stiffened his resolve to have only thoughts of Sally Lou. Prior to dressing, Johnson Perry vowed to leave today and begin the rest of his life with his true love who was waiting for his return.

Carrie began her new day more refreshed than expected after the commotion last night. She had already planned her day's work when she told Johnson the coffee was ready. During breakfast, she announced to him that she was going to wash his clothes as soon as it warmed up a little outside. Their morning conversation was less strained than last night. Maybe being fully clothed was the difference.

But that was not the main reason for a calmness that changed to an exciting stirring of their emotions. It was becoming more like a child's excitement before Christmas. As for Johnson, this calmness was like a tingle encompassed with a thrill, effervescing into an enigmatic feeling. A child had an idea what to expect. For him, the anticipation was unfamiliar and puzzling, but for some reason, he didn't want it to leave him. When he looked at Carrie this morning, her deep brown eyes didn't seem so hypnotic. They were more erotically appealing, and he could look at her longer before redirecting his eyes.

While milking and feeding the animals, he repeatedly convinced his mind and heart to leave in the early afternoon. First, however, he had to butcher the bear, help with heating the wash water, and fix the pantry door. He had planned his day's work and was leaving for sure after fixing the fence. Each of the nearly hundred times last night's image of Carrie paraded through his mind, he somehow managed to control aching desire from dominating his thoughts. He worked fast, and the fence was mended when she called him for lunch.

The two friends were more talkative at lunch than at breakfast.

"Johnson, I will cut your hair after we eat. You need to look your best when you get home."

Carrie's words were soft, and her demeanor was mannerly—but it wasn't a question. His eyes darted in her direction, and a slight head movement sealed his acceptance of her statement.

Most of the table talk was to and about Jane. Johnson took her while the table was cleared. He thanked the cook again and again for the dried beans and the leftover grits fried in butter. Plenty of biscuits were also leftover from breakfast. He told Carrie he was going to split some wood before his haircut. (He needed some time to think.)

The progress he achieved while outside, to resist Carrie's alluring attractiveness, was lost when she touched him. As she cut his hair, her hand would brush his neck or touch his ear. When she stood in front of him, he wanted to gather her in his arms. He came close—but didn't. He knew something was happening. The word "amour" wasn't in his vocabulary, but the foundation for a love affair, of an illicit and secret nature, was formed last night. He was now fighting something harder than any battle during the past two years. It was difficult to keep Sally Lou foremost in his mind.

After his hair was cut, Carrie said with a hint of gladness, "Your clothes won't be dry for another hour or so." At that instant, an axiom of self-evident truth infused the warm air in the cabin. Carrie was silently saying, "I know you are leaving today, but you can be with me for one more hour."

Earlier, Johnson was anxious to leave right after lunch, but now it didn't seem to matter when he left. A transformation in their relationship was occurring that neither could control. Two lonely years for Carrie and two terrible years for Johnson were suddenly only a vapor. They were acknowledging guilty thoughts and sending them to "it never happened land." Sally Lou's inhibiting influence was misty at best. The naked truth of physical attraction was intermittently being transmitted between two pairs of hungry, lustful eyes. A recording angel noted this. Something was going to happen. It was

like anticipating a looming afternoon storm, not knowing what degree of damage or what degree of pleasure
was coming from forces beyond their control.

Instead of going outside to split wood or doing
something inside the cabin, Johnson sat in *his* rocking
chair. Carrie picked up Jane and sat in the other rocker.
For the next few minutes, maybe five, neither spoke.
It seemed that time had either stopped or at least had
slowed. Being together seemed more important than
being separated. Carrie jerked when Johnson asked
about the Yankees who broke into the cellar. After a
brief recovery period, she began.

"Well let's see, it was two weeks ago. I happened to
be inside the cellar when one of the varmints walked
in and started to grab me. You know the room ain't
too big, and soon as he blocked the light coming in the
door, he was at me. I was at the table tending to my milk
crocks. He moved fast, but I moved faster. I had a crock
of milk in my hands when I felt his presence. Without
hesitating, I spun around and put that crock square in
his ugly face with all my strength. He fell backward. In
another quick movement, I grabbed his gun from his
belt and shot him between the eyes.

Lucky for me and Jane there was only two. Both came
in the front door of the cabin and out the pantry door.
After I shot the first one between the eyes, the second
one rushed out the pantry door. I shot him in the heart

with my derringer."

Only the soft murmuring of the crackling fire was heard as Johnson digested what he just heard. His mind drifted back two nights ago and realized she would have shot him had he made any move toward her.

"What happened to the bodies?

"Okay, this happened in daylight. When it got dark, I put a rope around Polly's neck, and drug them one at a time down the road and pushed them in a ditch. The next morning, I smoothed out where I drug them. The ground was froze and there wert much of a trail."

"Did someone find the bodies?"

"I haven't heard anybody say. But I've only talked to Flossie and Granger since I put them there. They live between here and Clifton Forge. Granger cuts and delivers wood blocks to me that I split before you came. Okay, I drug them the other way. I hauled little loads of dirt in my wagon for a week to cover them. I use the wagon to haul my eggs and butter and Jane to the store."

Both were relieved after this conversation. It was an antidote for what each was previously thinking. As least it was for Johnson.

CHAPTER 7

" . . . would you . . . do . . . do me a favor?"

After a long period of silence, Johnson stammered, "Carr . . . Carr . . . Carrie, I need . . . need to go."

"I know."

More silence.

"I will return these clothes."

"No need to—Earl don't need them."

There was stiffness in their conversation. Neither wanted to put words into action. Neither wanted to move out of their rocking chairs. But sometimes, fate makes hard decisions easy. Carrie suddenly fairly screamed to her mute chair mate.

"Johnson! It's snowing! I'll get your clothes off the line."

"I'll bring in more wood."

Carrie was back in the cabin first. She was standing at the fireplace when Johnson came in with an armload of wood. He put the wood down and then stood beside her—close. Neither spoke. They were getting used to their new agreement—he was staying another night. They both knew it could be longer, depending on the snow. In a second, the composure of two nervous strangers changed from indecisiveness to a relaxed state of contentment. The windows were small, but they could see big, fluffy snowflakes floating on a slight southwest wind. The snow of two nights ago had melted, and the ground was still too warm for this afternoon snow to accumulate. By morning, an inch or a foot could be on the ground. Carrie said she was afraid to predict since she missed snow signs this morning.

Johnson stood on the front porch and looked at the drifted snow that was too deep for walking. The wind was almost as fierce as the night he came to Carrie's cabin, and it now was much colder than when the snow started yesterday. His mind was having trouble remembering how many days and nights he had been in the cabin. During the past two years, his life had been focused solely on returning home to marry Sally Lou. This cold morning, standing on Carrie's front porch in his underwear, he was glad about the deep snow. Even with confusion howling in his head, he was glad he was not starting home today. He remembered many mornings during the war when his head seemed ready to burst thinking about where he was and how far he was from home. So many times he would have gladly begun walking.

It did not occur to him until he was back inside that this was his third morning with Carrie. He had arrived late Saturday night. Sunday was the first full day and he began moving the outhouse. Sunday night was bear night. Monday, he butchered the bear and finished the outhouse. Last night was his third night in the cabin. It was really his second night being a normal man. It was now Tuesday morning—the beginning of his third full day.

Johnson dressed and had just walked out the door to milk the cows when Carrie called him back.

Before going on with the story, let's return to Monday when the snow began.

After the sight of snowflakes changed Johnson's plan to leave, three happy people enjoyed a delightful afternoon. Carrie asked Johnson if he would play with Jane while she started supper. Carrie was mixing the crust for a blackberry cobbler when she began singing, "Carry me back to old Virginy—"

Johnson interrupted, Carrie! That's beautiful. I didn't know you could sing. You're really good."

He joined her, and she told him he had a great voice. Together, they sang many Stephen Foster songs and other songs including "Dixie," "Homespun Dress," "Yellow Rose of Texas," "Polly Wolly Doodle" and "Annie Laurie." Johnson sang "Goober Peas" and "Rose of Alabamy." Carrie sang "Darling Nelly Gray." The singing filled their hearts with a merriment that had them buoyantly free-floating above any guilt for recent thoughts. All the time supper was being prepared, it was song after song. Jane was content with Johnson, and the two adults were content with singing and having a carefree happy time. The meal was especially good and was crowned with blackberry cobbler and snow cream.

By evening milking time, the ground was white. What a different type of day for two young people who met three days ago during a snowstorm. It was snowing again, and the reluctance of leaving was quickly changed to relief.

An afternoon of levity had coalesced two hearts into an amiable bouquet of friendship. In addition to singing and food preparation, Carrie had been busy with her other chores, including churning milk and making butter. Jane had been active with Johnson and was ready for bed early. She had continually giggled and jabbered and had Carrie and Johnson chuckling when not singing.

Carrie sat beside Johnson by the fire after Jane was asleep. Low whistling sounds from blowing wind made the cabin more cozy than eerie. Occasional puffs of smoke would belch from the fireplace when a gust of cold wind rushed down the chimney. There was no moonlight tonight—just one coal oil lamp and flickering yellow blades of fire from the fireplace. A timorous boy and a girl sat four feet apart. The same two who earlier sang and laughed for hours were now quiet. Silent in deep thought, just like when the snow started. Something beautiful definitely happened today. During the afternoon, a storm did arrive. Gusts of passion encircled two lonely hearts bringing them dangerously (or happily) closer together. They were presently in the clam center of a whirlwind, and neither wanted to escape.

The cabin was warm and homey. Carrie was thinking that the three were just like a family. Another puff of smoke settled about their feet. Still looking at the fire, Carrie broke the silence with soft but strained words.

"Johnson, tell me about how you met Sally Lou."

He immediately turned toward her—how cruel to ask such a question. Ashamed and humiliated for not having Sally Lou foremost in his mind, he dropped his head and looked at the hot coals. He was suddenly as hot as the coals. All day, he tried to keep Sally Lou on his mind. But it was Carrie who had occupied his thoughts. He wasn't comparing the two, but did admit that he was more comfortable with Carrie than with Sally Lou. Carrie was more ardent, more spirited, and livelier. He was ready to explode when Carrie whispered, "That's okay, you don't need to talk about it." She decided to do the talking.

"I've already told you that we moved here from Wytheville in 1860 when I was fourteen. I met Earl when I was fifteen in the summer of 1861. It was at a dance and he walked me home. He was a nice enough person but not as kind and considerate as you."

Carrie stopped—waiting for any comment. Johnson said nothing.

"We were . . . well . . . guess we were courtin'. I didn't really like him all that much, but we had some fun times together. I was young and didn't . . . well, guess I didn't know what I wanted in life. After being alone for two years, my outlook on life is now different. Guess I mean with my wit and strength I've been able to survive and protect Jane and now know more of what I want."

Carrie had delivered this little dissertation in a soft, reflective manner while staring at the fire. She didn't say what she wanted in life but continued with her dialogue.

"Earl was drafted June 1862, and came home on furlough in February 1863. I've told you my parents died in January and being lonely was why I married Earl in February when I was sixteen. He said he would be home in a few months. Well, he didn't come back, but Jane came the following November."

In the short time Carrie was talking, Johnson's struggle with his shameful conscience had moderated until he could at least think about Sally Lou from another perspective. He had already talked about Sally Lou with respect to her being the reason he survived the war. Now, he guessed Carrie just wanted a factual account about how he met the girl he was going to marry. Without a prelude, Johnson began as if in a hurry get off this subject.

"We met while I was working in the hay field. Well, that was the first time I saw her. She has the prettiest red hair and real light or fair skin. I guess it's called complexion."

Stopping for a breath, he continued slower and softer.

"I didn't see her close until three days later at her house. I worked for her dad and had lunch with the family. She had two younger sisters and now a baby brother. We were both eighteen when we met. Her next younger sister, Meg, was sixteen and I think Patty was thirteen or fourteen. I remember Patty being real active. She liked to play jokes and make people laugh."

Johnson rested his case. She asked and he obliged—he honored her request. His thoughts now were neither more of Carrie nor more of Sally Lou. His mind was stabilized. He was ready for some sleep and then go home and let the time with Carrie be a fond memory. Talking about Sally Lou had actually made him more determined to return to her.

After more silence, Carrie soberly asked, "Will you tell me about where you live?"

They had not talked much since being together. He had stayed outside almost all daylight hours. Their conversation times had been more forced than comfortable except for this afternoon. Tenseness was again affecting their relationship. This was true for Johnson. Carrie seemed more relaxed than a few minutes earlier. Firelight polished her creamy complexion to a radiant luster. Her eyes sparkled, and again he was being siphoned into a dominion of weakness. But thoughts of home reinforced his promise to return. In an instant, temptation changed to resolve. He would answer her question and then go to bed.

"Falling Springs is the post office. Dad has a five hundred-acre farm two miles sorta north of the general store and post office. Falling Springs is located about fifteen miles north of Lewisburg. In 1850, the Lewisburg and Marlin Bottom Turnpike was finished. The whole area north of Lewisburg is one big fertile valley. It's a beautiful place to live. I've missed the farm and my family so much. I should be there now."

The magic circulating about the cabin this afternoon was disappearing. Carrie could feel a gulf between her and Johnson, though she never really had a claim on him. She painfully remembered his first statement when he arrived was to get home and marry Sally Lou. Even when her parents were living, there was never as much happiness in the cabin as this afternoon. She tightened her lips and almost cried while admitting to herself she loved this kind man sitting beside her. Maybe the happy time today was all she could expect with Johnson. Despite all the discipline that was a part of her rugged pioneer heritage, a tear slid down her face.

Without even a goodnight, Carrie abruptly went behind her hanging sheet. Johnson could hear her taking off her clothes, and his body quickened to an exciting fervor never before experienced. He quickly went to his floor pallet. A few minutes after Johnson reclined, Carrie stood in front of the fireplace and politely asked, "Johnson . . . would you . . . do . . . do me a favor?"

He acquiescently answered, "Yes."

As soon as he answered, he remembered the times he had volunteered while in the Army. Each time, he vowed not to do it again. But each new request was for something he believed would get him home quicker. The way Carrie asked made him say "yes" without thinking, but nothing she could want would prevent him from leaving for home tomorrow or the next day.

"Well, I was won . . . wondering if you cou . . . could hold me for a minute before I go back to bed? You see, I've been so lonely for so long that if you could just . . . just hold me fo . . . for a minute?"

Johnson raised up from his pallet and looked in awe at Carrie as she stood in her nightgown. Several times this afternoon, he was tempted to gather her in his arms and kiss away all her two years of loneliness. But he too had discipline, thick in his veins, that was a gift from many generations of his determined ancestors. Dueling forces were at battle in his subconscious—his pledge to Sally Lou and his physical desire for Carrie. In an instance of rebellion, he felt bridled to an unfair agreement with his promise to return. After all, he was almost home, and his pledge to Sally Lou had already worked its magic. He was safe and sound minus one foot.

When Johnson first saw the dim cabin light, he didn't know, three days later, he would be confronted with a burden of this magnitude. He had always been a good moral person and obedient to his word. The wind was suddenly louder or was his head ready to explode. He was getting warm. He couldn't remember any time in battle when he felt this way. He was trained to fight—

to charge and subdue the enemy. Carrie was definitely not the enemy but was waiting for an answer. He didn't know what he was going to say until he spoke.

"Oh no, no I ca . . . can't . . . oh no. I've nev . . . never . . . no . . . I've never been . . . been close to a wo . . . woman in a nightgown."

Beads of perspiration covered his brow. He expended more energy saying those few words than he had during a battlefield charge screaming the Rebel Yell. What was she saying—what was she asking? In his mind he knew, but in his heart he knew Sally Lou was waiting for him.

"That's okay—I shouldn't have asked. It's been so long since I've felt the strong arms of a man around me. I am so proud of you Johnson. You have protected me and Jane. It's been a delightful day—you know with the singing and the snow and with Jane being so happy. But I shouldn't have asked."

By the inflection of her voice, he knew it was not okay. She wanted a man's arms around her—his arms. Most of the day, Johnson had not thought about Sally Lou. He was lost in the happiness shared with Carrie. During the past few ticks of time, he wanted to be close to these beautiful, fascinating one hundred pounds of desire. He wanted to do more than just hold her in his arms. These were his thoughts as he stood by his pallet.

The wind changed to a forlorn wail. The cabin was suddenly chilled as if the fire needed another log. Johnson's mind was tumbling between honor of his word and a walk down a road never traveled. He didn't know that roads of this nature often have an abyss too deep to measure. He didn't know (yet) that amorous love could bring a man to his knees begging for another embrace. But Johnson was not going to enfold his arms around Carrie. Before he could think anymore about what he was not going to do, she took three steps toward him. She was inches from a strong, fearless man who suddenly was so weak and scared, he would have slumped to the floor if she had not enfolded her arms around him. In an instinctive move, Johnson gathered Carrie into his arms. Both trembled as the blackness of the abyss wrapped around them until only touch and feel registered in their fervent minds.

Carrie had two nightgowns. She was wearing the one with buttons on the front. The top two buttons were in place. The next four were unbuttoned. Maybe Carrie's next move was premeditated due to Johnson's closeness during the day—maybe her next move was daringly executed because her love for him was ready to explode within if she didn't surrender to the message from her heart. Nevertheless, in a fluid motion, Carrie rotated within Johnson's quivering arms. In another graceful movement, she placed his right hand on her abdomen. Her man wanted to pull it back, but didn't. She was so warm and soft. Before he could decide what to do next—if anything, she slowly moved his hand to her breasts.

Johnson Perry, by a carnal, deliberate command from his subconscious began a charge down a road never traveled. His intimidating Rebel Yells of recent past would become whimpering moans as Carrie's clinging arms and legs squeezed out the most pleasant feeling he had ever known.

It was far more than physical. Even though Johnson didn't know the meaning of "physiologic," his mind and body could feel such effects by knowing someone affectionately cared for him in a way like never before.

Honor First

CHAPTER 8

Five minutes later . . .

Five minutes later, they were side by side in bed. Johnson was still disoriented from a charge down a road he never dreamed would take him to a place that must have been Heaven. He tried hard not to cry, but happy tears streamed down his flushed face. Carrie cried too, and their warm tears mingled as she kissed his face while repeating, "I love you, I love you, I love you . . . "

It took another couple of minutes before breathing had modulated close to normal. But then Mr. Perry wasn't sure he would ever be normal again. In a move that would be repeated many times, Carrie rolled over to Johnson and placed her left leg between his legs as she put her head on his hairy chest. For another five minutes, neither moved. While still coated with stardust, Johnson's second expression of love for Carrie lasted seven minutes. When Carrie finally recovered, she placed her left leg between her lover's legs and put her head on his chest. Now it was time for sleep.

One, two, three or four hours later (neither knew or cared), they made love for the third time. Johnson's kisses were unexpected but were passionately returned. During their first "flyaway," his intrinsic instinct guided him through those initial uncharted moments. During their second flight, he whispered so many sweet words along the way that she flew out of her mind two times.

When she became aware she was back in bed, her body was so glorified, that she was sure a part of her was still in their enchanted paradise. She wondered if other women had ever been to that empyreal firmament where you can feel the brush of angel hair on your face. Carrie didn't know what that big hunk of a man beside her was thinking—he was quiet and seemed to be content. She concluded he needed a kiss, and then she placed her left leg between his legs and put her head on his chest—her new sleepy-time position.

It was ten the next morning when Johnson finally decided he had been with Carrie four days. His thoughts all morning had been about last night and early this morning. After the rooster crowed, their levitation through the cabin rafters before breakfast was no less glorious than the three other visits to "pleasantville." While he milked and fed the animals, Carrie fixed a tall stack of flapjacks for her man. After that, "Her Man" sat in his rocker and watched Jane most of the morning. The snow had stopped but not until ten inches accumulated on the fallow ground.

After lunch, Johnson rocked Jane to sleep. Carrie asked if he would also like to take a nap. She was in bed first. In a gesture now familiar to Johnson, she placed her left leg between his legs and her head on his chest. Instead of relaxing before sleep, she spoke with a guise of seriousness. "Johnson," She paused while squeezing his hand. "Johnson, can I tell you something personal?"

He replied immediately, "Now wait a minute Miss Carrie. We've only knowed each other four days. Just because we have been and been and been to Heaven Land with your arms and legs wrapped around me—just because we have cried, moaned and screamed together, is no reason to get personal. Just because you sent me to a place so beautiful that I can't much think of anything else—just because you had me tumbling in space till my mind and body exploded, is no reason to get personal. But each time, I was blessed when pieces were put back together, and you were clinging to me like a drowning victim."

Johnson stopped when he realized his clinging partner was crying. He gently pulled her up until he could kiss her tear-soaked face. He savored each salty tear on her beautiful face until they again soared out of their minds.

If they really intended to nap, it didn't happen. Once back on planet Earth, and in a favorite position, Carrie pointedly told Johnson she was going to tell him something personal.

"When I was married to Earl, I knew nothing like we have shared. I was scared, and he was anxious. We—I should say *he*—did it several times a day. He said he was going to take advantage of his furlough and his honeymoon. I had all the chores to do, which included three meals each day, and I was never ready for him. He would not even milk the cows. He did carry in firewood that I had split."

Carrie stopped for a few heartbeats to organize her thoughts and then continued with a slower delivery.

"I could pretty much say he was either in bed with me or in bed alone resting or sleeping. What I'm trying to say—you and me flew at the same time to that paradise place where we were breathless until we floated back to Earth in each other's arms. I'm telling you, my love, you were my first real lovin' man. Do you understand?"

"Could you repeat that?"

Carrie shouted, "Oh Johnson! I'm serious. Don't you understand?"

"Right now, all I understand and care about is . . . " He paused and then shouted louder, "I LOVE YOU!"

Before the beautiful girl in his arms could respond, Jane awoke.

CHAPTER 9

Sally Lou was someone he used to know.

Johnson's fifth day with Carrie began as a cold Thursday, but the sun was soon melting the snow. He had been splitting wood for two hours when Carrie called, saying she needed him. Since he was in her clinging web, he would do anything she asked.

"Would you taste this blackberry cake?"

In humble obedience to the one he loved more than he could express, he tasted and judged.

"There's something—let me taste again."

While reaching for a third piece, Carrie interrupted and kissed him until he waved his arms for her to let him breathe. This started another round of laughing and cat and mouse tactics. When they realized they were locked in two pairs of arms and both were having trouble breathing, a little seriousness prevailed. For two days, they had giggled and frolicked about in and out of the cabin. Carrie told her playmate she had never had so much fun throwing snowballs.

Later, while seated in his rocker, Johnson couldn't remember when he last thought of Sally Lou. She was with him all right, but in a catacomb of his mind. Somehow it seemed acceptable that she was in second place. His thoughts were with the present—with Carrie and her love for him. When he did think of the girl back home, reminiscent scenes were blurry and seemed so long ago. He didn't think about the many times she had been an inspiration for him to survive the war. He was, however, troubled when he was aware that Sally Lou was waiting for him to return.

Sometimes in a cloud of misty feelings, he longed for even a minuscule vestige of guidance to help him decide what to do. The few times he tried to concentrate on Sally Lou, Carrie would say something or come into view or kiss him. So, his first love was again repositioned to his second or backup love. For some reason, this didn't bother him, and he didn't know why. The love he had shared with Carrie had been so intense that his previous, logical thinking ability had been reduced to thinking only of the next moment with his little gal.

The rest of the day for Johnson was total contentment. There was an idyllic ambience in the cabin. His love for Carrie was greater than any previous delightful thought of love. She was pampering him by never letting him get his coffee or tea. She would stand behind him and rub his neck and back. She ran her fingers through his hair often. She kissed him often. His spirits ratcheted higher each time she touched him. He had never imagined such a degree of ardor and passion.

The snow had melted some but was still too deep to begin his homeward journey. He even had some weird thoughts he was home. Sally Lou was someone he used to know. His mind had changed course. He was in a placid and serene dimension because his heart was at the helm. His happy heart had his tingling body anchored in deep waters. Supper was another blue-ribbon meal. Carrie was young, but her meals had presentation, texture and taste. Her visitor could add—and quantity. He had gained enough weight that Earl's pants were a perfect fit in the waist.

When Jane was asleep, the two lovers sat in their respective rocking chairs. The fire was particularly cheery tonight. As they sat in silence, no doubt, they had some fleeting thoughts about their time locked in each other's arms. Johnson's mind was burning when he turned and smiled at his five-foot-two beauty. She returned his smile, and he had to quickly divert his eyes. Her intense black eyes seemed to penetrate to his brain. He recovered and spoke, not looking at her.

"I'm going to tell you my private thoughts. I love you Carrie Butler."

"Can you prove it?"

All she heard was the hissing and crackling sounds from the fire, until the sweetest words she had ever heard were uttered from her Prince Charming, sitting four feet from away.

"If I stayed here would that prove it?"

"What! What do you mean . . . you mean forever?"

"No."

"I don't understand." Carrie was perplexed. Her face was showing part frown and part disbelief.

"I mean longer than forever—until the end of time, and then we would start over again. I love you more than—"

Johnson never finished his proclamation. Carrie moved in front of him—on her knees. With her head in his lap, she cried until she was limp.

They were in bed a little later and were soon in flight to a destination beyond the Milky Way. Carrie was so excited about her man wanting to stay, she gloriously flew the circuit two times. After a short rest, they were at it again. This time, Carrie's scream woke Jane.

Johnson was still asleep when it was time for their after midnight session. Carrie gently kissed her man, who had given her more love in four nights than some women probably receive in a lifetime.

Her man suddenly rose up, knocking her to the side. With a wild look in his eyes, he screamed, "SALLY LOU! SALLY LOU! I'm coming . . . I'm coming."

He then looked at Carrie with a frantic expression. He blinked his eyes while looking at her. She was puzzled—he was bewildered. When he reclined, she moved to him and noticed he was perspiring. She reversed her motion until her back was toward him. Her pillow was soon wet with burning tears. Johnson didn't fully awaken but would surely remember his dream—her nightmare.

Before her pain was subdued, she remembered each hour with Johnson. She remembered how she felt when she heard the gun shot out back. She especially remembered the first time she saw that cold, hungry soldier boy and the first time his arm encircled her. The next day was Friday and he would be leaving. Carrie always appreciated the few gifts she had received. The happy time with Johnson would be her most cherished one, for this could never happen again.

CHAPTER 10

"...I know why you're leaving me."

When the rooster crowed, Carrie was already awake—had been for a long time. She had been thinking about what she could have done differently that could possibly change what was going to happen later. Last night when he announced his perpetual love, she should have realized Sally Lou was to the side of his mind and not out of it completely. When he arrived, she knew Sally Lou was his focus. But what can one do when a lonely heart defies a discerning mind? She had always believed her mind to be wise and shrewd, but a force greater than her discerning intent overpowered her resolute way of thinking. On winds of desire, she had rushed into his heart like a fool. Now, she was relinquished to reaping the proverbial whirlwind.

She quietly slipped out at the foot of the bed and started coffee. When Johnson opened his eyes, she was sitting by the fire. Her thoughts were a bit different than when sitting here last night.

While still in bed, he humbly spoke, "I had a dream last night."

"I know."

"How could you know?"

"I was awake when you cried out her name and said you were coming to her."

Johnson closed his eyes so not to see the hurt on Carrie's face. In an effort to justify his forthcoming announcement, he explained his dream.

"Carrie . . . in my dream, Sally Lou was in some kind of trouble or pain or something that caused her to need me."

"Johnson, I understand." She added in her mind, "I need you, too."

"But will you or can you believe me when I say this morning that I'll always love you Carrie?"

"I do and understand why you have to leave today."

There—she had said it. With his decision known, he joined her by the fire. He had dreaded her presence, but she had subjugated his fears—she had routed his apprehension by saying he was leaving today.

Pensively, Carrie said, "I will fix some food."

"You don't need to . . . "

"But I want to. You will appreciate it later."

"Yes I guess so. Thank you."

Normally, Carrie would be busy in the kitchen with breakfast. But she was having a second cup of strong coffee. She needed something extra this morning if she was going to survive his leaving.

While priority chores were attended to. Jane was especially playful, which helped to smooth the solemn expression on two adult faces. The magic that once sauntered about the cabin was now cloistered in the wall cracks. The air was sober and listless. Every smile was forced.

The snow was too deep for comfortable walking, but it was time to go. They both knew the sooner the better. Extra biscuits and bacon were prepared for a solo journey far different from the recent hugging, moaning excursions they had taken together.

Two unhappy hearts were realigning thoughts to cope with an imminent odyssey paved with reality. Neither belonged to the other. Deep down they knew this, but for some sweet twists of time, they had ascended to angel land. They were repeatedly bathed in stardust as they flew through, and beyond, the Milky Way—lovely memories that could never be dusted from their minds.

It happened so quickly. A flurry of packing had Jane confused. She wanted to play with her new friend.

Carrie earlier vowed not to cry anymore. When his arms were around her, tears came from a spring she thought was dry. Johnson could feel her breasts pressing on his chest. They were clinging to each other as they had oft before, but a dull throbbing in their hearts was replacing the extreme joy of recent days. Numbness flashed through Johnson's body. For a moment, he thought he would collapse. When she looked up, her face was flushed and skewed with pain. He pulled her close again—he couldn't bear to see her so unhappy. Before he exploded or collapsed, he forced out some parting words.

"Carrie . . . last night, I . . . I meant what I said about lovin' you longer than forever. But I gave my word before I met you. I . . . I need to honor my word. I was taught honor first, and then life can be enjoyed without shame and regret. A man has to be able to live with what he says he will do."

"I know . . . I know why you're leaving me."

Johnson hurried to say one more thing. "The soldiers will soon be coming back and you'll find a good man."

"I think so. I think Oliver Cochran likes me. His dad said he's coming home soon."

Carrie stood on her tiptoes and looked into Johnson's cheerless eyes. He squeezed her again until she couldn't breathe. The following kiss would not have won any prize for style or technique, but for a mutual expression of unmitigated love, it would have garnered the most glorious award angels had to offer. Along with their exchange of adoration for each other, they were letting guilt evaporate from within. Carrie knew it was wrong to be with Johnson without any hope to marry him. Johnson knew he shouldn't be with Carrie when Sally Lou was waiting for him. Superimposed on their sadness was a measure of gladness for terminating what they knew was wrong with respect to God's law.

The embrace seemed much longer than a minute. Johnson reluctantly backed away, turned, walked out of Carrie's cabin and out of her life. As he walked through the snow, she called to him from the porch.

"Johnson . . . I love you, and you'll stay on my mind. I will never forget you."

The young, discharged soldier, walking away from what could have been the greatest chapter in his life, didn't stop or turn his head. His body and mind were presently in more torment than at any other time in his life. He was torn between his word of honor to Sally Lou and his love for Carrie. But last night's dream was so real that he had no choice—Sally Lou was waiting for him.

Later, Carrie would repeatedly see, in her mind, a trail of shoe prints and small holes in the snow. Later, Johnson would repeatedly see, in his mind, two dark brown eyes glistening with tears as Carrie looked up at him for the last time.

CHAPTER 11

. . . *back home again.*

A thousand thoughts a mile occupied Johnson's mind as he plodded homeward. He missed Carrie more than he wanted to admit. He missed the warm cabin and her warm, clinging body. After two days on the road, he still wanted to do an about-face and march back into her loving arms. Three times he had turned, but only for a short distance, before his promise to Sally Lou turned his heart homeward.

The snow had melted by the fourth day, and traveling was easier. Daytime temperatures ranged in the forties and fifties. Each lonely mile, Johnson tried to spin Carrie from his mind. If he had not seen her cabin light—if it had not snowed so much, he would not have met her. So many ifs, and what he did and shouldn't have done, were depressing him until his head seemed ready to explode. But he felt good about the money.

He gave her two hundred Virginia Confederate dollars and told her to spend it fast. He told her about overhearing two officers say that the war couldn't last much longer. After some discussion about the war and inflated prices, Carrie took the soon to be worthless money. A paltry smile embellished his brooding face when he remembered saying he had eaten more butter and eggs than what the money could fetch.

Just after noon on Monday, the tenth day after leaving Carrie, Johnson Perry was back home again. The homecoming was jubilant. His mother's first concern after greeting her son, was to feed him. She was certainly pleased to see him eat so much. He scarcely talked while eating. When asked about his trip home, Johnson said it was cold and snowy but otherwise uneventful. He meant the last ten days.

Sitting by the fire, he told them about his leg and a little about his illnesses. He had not been home since leaving two years earlier, and he missed his family the same as Sally Lou. Being the same kind, obedient child his parents knew, he gave them the respect they deserved before asking about Sally Lou.

"Have you seen Sally Lou lately?"

Gathered around the fire were his Mom and Dad, sister Lillie, brother Robert, and baby sister Rachel. In the last letter from his Mom, she told him about his brother, Sam, who would not be returning home from the war. The Confederate draft age was changed in February 1864, from 18-45 to 17-50. Sam was seventeen in June of 1864. His first battle was in Nashville, Tennessee in mid December 1864. He died a week later from a head wound received in the battle.

No one answered his question. His Mom was the first to speak. "Son, let me get you more coffee."

"No Mom—has Sally Lou been here lately?"

Still no one spoke. Johnson began to stand. His Dad put a hand on his shoulder and then reverently spoke.

"Son . . . No, Sally Lou has not been here lately."

Johnson didn't know how he did it, but as the lonely miles had trailed behind him, Carrie became someone he used to know, and Sally Lou became foremost in his mind. Visions of how Sally Lou motivated him to survive the war were like a company flag proudly carried into a battle. He had truly been in a battle with his conscience and what was right and wrong with his relationship with Carrie. He knew his love for Carrie would never be forgotten, but the nearer he got to home, the nearer he wanted to be to Sally Lou. He was tired and dirty and wanted to start planning the rest of his life.

The timbre in his Dad's voice alerted Johnson that something had happened.

"Will someone tell me about Sal . . . "

He began to shake and rub his hands together.

"Lillie, will you tell me what has happened to . . . "

Again, he couldn't say her name. After a few erratic heartbeats, Johnson quickly stood and looked at his mother and politely asked, "Mom, do I have any clean clothes? I'm going to bathe and . . . "

Father Perry also stood and didn't speak as docilely as before. "Johnson! Sit down, and I will tell you what happened to Sally Lou."

Johnson was a man proven many times over, but he sat down as a little boy would when commanded by Dad. A nervous hush surrounded the Perry family before Andrew Lee Perry spoke.

"Son, your Sally Lou got sick and went to her rewards in Heaven." He paused, waiting for a reaction or more questions. His son didn't move his eyes from the fire. "Johnson, we laid her to rest, I think, ten days ago."

A cold chill rippled through Johnson's tired body as he realized she was buried the day he left Carrie's cabin. He wanted to evaporate—to just get out of this room. But he had to ask one more question.

"When . . . when did . . . did she . . . "

He was having trouble finishing sentences. His mom had made it a priority in her life to remember all birthdays, marriages, and deaths for miles around.

"Johnson, she took her last breath Thursday night, the thirtieth of March. We put her to rest the next day, Friday the thirty-first of March in this year of our Lord, 1865."

He gripped the chair arms, and his lips disappeared as he tried to hold back some bitter tears. A small part of his mind was sane enough to know she died the night he had that disturbing dream. He tried to decide—had he not stopped at Carrie's cabin for six days, would he have been home before she . . . He couldn't figure out if it would have mattered. His head was burning as hot as the fire.

The children left the room when the tears started. His mother, Lola Mae, walked behind him and kindly said, "It's all right to cry. It's okay to let the hurt come out. She was a . . . She would come over to check if we heard from you."

With all his willpower, he slowed the tears and asked in choppy words, "When . . . was . . . was she here last?"

His mother didn't answer for a few seconds.

"Well son, I don't rightly know."

Johnson thought it strange his mother couldn't remember about Sally Lou's last visit but never forgot a birthday, marriage, or funeral date. He didn't query further.

He recovered from this shock quicker than he thought possible and told his mom he was going to bathe and go to bed. "I haven't slept much lately."

Johnson was tired but didn't drift to sleep until just before dawn. What he heard about Sally Lou circulated in his mind until he wanted to scream. He couldn't believe this was happening to him.

After breakfast, he asked Lillie to walk with him to the cabin. Lillie was sixteen and a good friend of Sally Lou's younger sister, Patty, who was either fifteen or sixteen. Lillie had looked at his leg, as did the other family members, with both sorrow and fascination. But his handicap was accepted as a blessing because most of him returned.

At breakfast, he had announced he was going to make a new peg, and he could then walk much better. After a period of silence, he asked how Sally Lou passed.

His mother answered, "She come down with too–ber–ca . . . ca . . . "

Lillie quickly said, "Tuberculosis." She always admired her big brother and was thrilled he asked her to be with him. They were kindred-spirit siblings and had spent many compatible hours together. But Johnson had an alternative motive for asking Lillie to walk with him.

The cabin needed some repair. Brother Robert would seldom visit the cabin and had not made any repairs. He was not an outdoor type of person. He did chores and helped with other farm work grudgingly. His passion in life was reading and writing. Johnson and Sam, the brother who wasn't coming back home, built the cabin when they were twelve and ten. Lillie wasn't allowed to come here alone, but she and Patty had been here on a few Sunday afternoons.

Johnson talked about when he and Sam built the cabin. He told her that Sam was his best friend and will always be missed. In the middle of a story that happened while building the cabin, Johnson stopped and said, "Well Lillie, I need to repair our cabin. I think Sam would like that."

Lillie didn't comment.

"What you say we start back?"

She was wondering why he hadn't asked about Sally Lou. She knew why she was invited. She didn't have to wait long.

"Lillie, tell me what happened."

"Oh Johnson, I have cried till I got sick—so did Patty. I saw her two days ago and we cried together till we about passed out."

"Did she suffer . . . I mean long?"

Lillie put her arms around Johnson and cried until he began crying. He led her to a large rock under a hickory tree. He did his strap thing and they sat down. The air was cold, but the sun was warm enough for them to feel comfortable. Lillie partially recovered and began in soggy words.

"She . . . she . . . got married ten months— "

Johnson flinched and screamed, "WHAT! What do you . . . you . . . ?"

He couldn't finish. Both were silent for a long time. He didn't know what to think. When he was discharged, it had been seven months since a letter. But that had happened one other time because of his moving around and mail being slow. The last letter from Sally Lou was dated June the first, which he received in the middle of July. Nothing in the letter indicated she was even thinking about marriage.

Strangely, he hadn't thought of Carrie for more than a second at a time since returning home. Right now, his mind was blank—except he couldn't believe Sally Lou would not wait for him. This was a worse shock than when he knew about his leg. When his breathing slowly returned to near normal, Johnson asked, "Will you tell me more?"

"This man came to Lewisburg and saw Sally Lou when she was there with her dad. While her dad was seeing a man about some cows, this man introduced himself. She told Patty nothing ever hit her so hard. Patty seen him once and said he wore the finest clothes. He came from out west and dressed like a cowboy. He wore a fancy jacket and snake-hide boots and a big white hat."

Johnson's chin almost touched his chest while listening about the one who gave him strength and courage to . . . he couldn't finish his thought.

"Patty said she sneaked out of the house after dark the fifteenth of June last year."

"When, or did, she come back home? Did she pass away at home or—?

Lillie put up her hand to stop him.

"Johnson, what happened is why Patty and me have cried so much. This man, we found out later was named Fred Lane, took her to Harrisonburg and later left her in September when she got sick. He left her alone. She almost died there. She didn't much know anybody. Some old lady got a man to come and see Mr. Foster. It was this past January when he got her home."

The sun got warmer, and Johnson stood up and removed his jacket. Not looking at Lillie, he asked, "So she was home three months?"

"Almost—it was around the second week in January when she come home."

"Couldn't the doctor make her well?"

"Patty said she heard the doctor talking to her daddy, and the doc said she was the worst case he had seen. I don't know, but I guess the doctor did all he could."

"She's been gone eleven . . . no, twelve days?"

"I think that's right."

"Guess we should get back."

CHAPTER 12

"...I'll be sixteen in two weeks."

Johnson spent the rest of his second day home in the blacksmith shop, working on a new peg. The design was complete in his mind, since he had thought about it a lot after leaving Carrie. Somewhere along the way, his thoughts switched from her to his peg design and to Sally Lou. Occasional thoughts of Carrie, however, would still send waves of pleasure through his body. In his mind, she would always be someone he would never forget, but he believed she would soon marry a local man. Now that Sally Lou was gone, he was free to return but for some reason had no intentions of seeing Carrie again. He guessed being back home again was the reason.

He was truly excited to be back home and energized to be in the shop. Before the war, he had become an able blacksmith and was anxious to begin his project. He first made a metal cup and riveted it on the side of a rather heavy metal bar. A piece of sheet metal, the shape of a shoe sole hinged near the middle, was fixed to the end of the bar. The cup was lined with a sheepskin to be soft for his stub. The sole-like metal was wrapped with many strips of leather to resemble a foot. The flexible strips would be a shock absorber as he walked. The heavy bar extended from the foot to just below his knee. Johnson's hand-fashioned prosthesis was attached to his leg with two leather straps. His device was finished as daylight faded.

As he walked to the house for supper, a neighbor rode by and told him Lee had surrendered to Grant last Sunday at Appomattox Court House. His family showed great gladness for the war's conclusion, but they expressed sadness for losing a son and for Johnson losing part of his leg and a foot. They talked about hardships during the past four years and about the uncertain future for both North and South. Similar conversations, no doubt, were ongoing throughout the southland. Their area had not been devastated like some of the South, but the war had taken a toll. So much had been wasted, and daily worry and the uncertain future were a heavy burden to carry.

Johnson's mother had just spoken that last sentence. He suddenly thought of Carrie when she said carry. He was reminded of the first song he heard her sing. The conversation lasted till bedtime, with Johnson contributing little. His mom and dad were justified, he thought, to talk about the war as the most terrible thing that had ever personally happened to them.

Johnson was in the blacksmith shop most of the next day, Wednesday, remaking the foot part of his prosthesis. It took three remakes before he could walk almost as naturally as before. The sole hinge was moved two times, but the most significant improvement was a hinge where the vertical bar and foot piece connected. Around the hinge, leather strips were tightly wrapped to restrict movement that substituted for ankle muscles. Most of his time was spent experimenting with the degree of stiffness to allow for an optimum step pattern.

When chores were completed, Johnson was feeling good on his first Thursday home after the war. He couldn't have been happier about his new foot while walking to visit the Fosters. He had to talk to Patty. He had to find out more. His thoughts were disconnected. He wanted to know why Sally Lou eloped—but then he didn't want to know. Nevertheless, he was almost there and almost cried when one of her favorite fragrances filled the air.

Patty saw him coming and met him with a smile. He remembered her being attractive, but the beauty before his eyes stopped him in his tracts. Could this be so in just two years? She was taller than Carrie but had the same color hair and dark brown eyes. So why was Carrie being used as a reference? He should have compared her with Sally Lou. Patty also, he would soon find, had a personality similar to Carrie's. Patty laughed and joked more than Sally Lou and Carrie, but he would also find later, this bubbling beauty had a serious side—a side that would change his life.

"Wow! Patty, you look great. Are you eighteen?"

"No Johnson, I'll be sixteen in two weeks."

Her admiration for him soared to know he thought she was as old as Sally Lou. Patty was not one to let a conversation stall.

"Well Johnson, you look great. I see you escaped the awful war without any missing parts."

In his letters home after his leg amputation, he didn't mention his injury. When his family first saw him, his condition was not unfamiliar to them. Many soldiers were returning home with missing parts. They were concerned, but understanding. Lillie couldn't tell Patty anything, because she hadn't known until a few days ago. They had not talked for a week.

"Oh, I'm okay."

Patty didn't apologize about not being dressed for company. All the time, she looked neat and beautiful. Her form-fitting dress showed her proportioned curves so well that Johnson had to force himself not to stare. He also feasted on her brown eyes and rosy cheeks.

After meeting the family, they walked toward the barn, and he softly asked, "Patty, tell me about—"

She didn't let him finish.

"Johnson." She paused trying to decide what to say first. Looking at the ground, she rubbed her hands together before saying, "Are you sure you want to know what happened?"

Without hesitation—"Yes."

"I don't care what you think of me, but I'm going to call him a SOB. I even think he's the devil for what he did. He sweet-talked her to believe that you were killed at Cold Harbor. He told her that almost all the Confederates were killed. He said you didn't have a chance to survive. I can't imagine why she would believe him."

"It so happened that I didn't get a scratch. I was wounded three times but not at Cold Harbor. I got a letter from her just before the battle that I'm sure got me through safe. She said she could hardly wait for us to be married."

Patty stared at Johnson. "Were your wounds bad? You look all right. I mean . . . I guess they healed."

"Yes they healed."

"I guess Lillie told most of what happened. But what I'm going to say next is what really hurts."

She looked to the house and then, while turning to face Johnson, blurted, "Daddy don't think she got married. He checked some and couldn't find no record. When she come home, he never asked her. She was so sick we didn't think she would last a week. We never did ask her anything about why she run away. Everybody was so glad to have her back home. We didn't know where she went until that man come to tell Daddy where she was and that she was bad sick."

Patty was quiet for what seemed like minutes to Johnson. She then began to cry. He waited for her to stop crying. When it appeared she wasn't going to stop, he moved closer and embraced her. They were in full view of the house, but neither cared who saw them. In muffled words, she said, "Sally Lou said that if you come back she wanted me to tell you that she was sorry for not waiting for you. She said the Lord has forgiven her and would hope you would."

Both were crying after that message. As they were holding on to each other, Patty finally told him those were her last words. "She could only whisper them and then she looked right at me with a faint smile before she was gone."

When the tears stopped, two sad people departed with different thoughts to ponder. Johnson's initial thought was that a chapter in his life had ended. With a man's arms around her for the first time, Patty's thoughts were of a new chapter in her life.

Saturday afternoon, Patty arrived at the Perry's to spend the night with Lillie.

CHAPTER 13

. . . a man of his word . . .

Carrie folded the tablet paper and put her head down on the table. It was her second anniversary—two months since she and Johnson first slept together. The first month of vapid days after he left was almost more than she could bear. She was not the busy person she had been all her life. Only the essential chores were completed, including some garden work. She knew that had to be done for her and Jane to have food. She often began something and would just stop and do nothing for hours. Jane received proper care, but beyond her baby's needs, Carrie muddled through listless days and nights.

Her thoughts were constantly on Johnson. She wanted to think there was nothing more she could have done to make him stay. She wanted to go after him. Her life was over. Sitting alone was now so much more difficult. Lonely days and nights were her unchanging companion. The sun would rise and set with regularity, unnoticed by a spiritless, brokenhearted girl of eighteen. She was living a twenty-four hour day with some light and some dark. She only slept a few hours at a time. She didn't know or care whether it was day or night. Her only schedule was milking two times a day.

She unfolded the paper and began to cry—again. A week ago, she composed a song, but she could only sing it at certain times. She had just written the words on paper. The tune was in her mind. After a short while (it was probably a *long* while, because lately time was measured in teardrops, and the paper was wet), she began humming. Only after another crying session could she sing the song.

I CAN'T FORGET YOU

1. I still cry myself to sleep
And dream that we're not through.
You stay on my mind
I can't forget you.

Lonely times are all I have
While you're with your Sally Lou.
You stay on my mind
I can't forget you.

CHORUS: *When I rest in peaceful sleep*
You will still stay on my mind.
And I'll dream of you
Throughout endless time.

I still miss the times we cried
And all the love we knew.
You stay on my mind
I can't forget you.

2. I pretend you will be back
In just a week or two.
You stay on my mind
I can't forget you.
Each new dawn I see your smile
Sprinkled with the morning dew.
You stay on my mind
I can't forget you.

CHORUS: *When I rest in peaceful sleep*
You will still stay on my mind.
And I'll dream of you
Throughout endless time.

I still miss the times we cried
And all the love we knew.
You stay on my mind
I can't forget you.

Johnson and Patty were together once or twice a week. He enjoyed her company and had to admit she mitigated the loss of Sally Lou. When he began spending time with Patty, she reminded him of Carrie, but that connection was steadily diminishing. Her friendship was becoming so pleasurable he didn't need to compare her with anyone else. She was witty and dangerously flirty. Johnson laughed more with Patty than with Carrie, but Carrie was more loving. But he guessed that was not a fair comparison—yet.

Johnson's thoughts about life had changed since returning home from the war. He had lived on the edge of death for most of his two years in the Army. He had done and had seen things so horrible, that for a while, he didn't think sleep would ever again be peaceful. He met Carrie and experienced a way of living so beautiful that many horrors of war were erased. But his unwavering determination to be a man of his word compelled him to make a heart breaking decision to leave Carrie and return to Sally Lou.

Looking back, he guessed a change began when he found out about Sally Lou—then the details. He was still pondering the forgiving part and was still sorting his thoughts, trying to arrange their value according to future importance. But when Patty entered his life as a surrogate for Sally Lou, his convictions began to seek a middle road. Her fun and careless ways stimulated a recent memory. He was thinking about a certain avenue without commitment. Patty was marrying age, but why enter into a covenant if one could have the icing without the encumbrance of the cake.

This comprised most of his thoughts while repairing the cabin, which he named Sam's Cabin. He had spent many happy hours restoring the cabin he and Sam built, what seemed like a hundred years ago.

CHAPTER 14

It was like a light flashed before his eyes.

Since Johnson's return home, his major work effort was in the blacksmith shop. Many of his dad's farm implements had not been properly repaired during the past two years. Other farmers had repair work that permitted him to make and save some money. He also helped with farm work that, in his mind, offset his room and board. Of course, his mother wouldn't think that way.

He still enjoyed Patty's company. When she would stay overnight with Lillie, she would help him work in the shop. Their parents knew they were courting and didn't object. Johnson would watch Patty as she operated the bellows at the forge. At times, the fire would illuminate her face and remind him of another time in his life. Sometimes, thoughts of Carrie would cause him to hammer a finger. Patty would kiss it, which only increased the pain in his lustful heart.

May ended with the promise of a good crop year. But pain and scars of the past four years daily reminded them their crop of dreams during that period was blighted almost to extinction.

In early June, Johnson bought a horse and a light wagon. He fitted the sides with two sets of brackets for spring seats. But he only made one seat, thus allowing for cargo space behind it.

Sunday afternoon, the fourth of June, Johnson and Patty walked to the cabin. Johnson had recently tasted the nectar of love, and his heart was making a beeline to the most beautiful flower in Greenbrier County. Patty was ready for Johnson to fill her body and soul with a love she had recently been expecting. Dark clouds suddenly billowed in the western sky. The first kiss in the cabin was soft and exciting. A second kiss sent Patty Foster tumbling, as if she were in the dark clouds.

Then there was noise—not thunder but Mr. Perry.

"Son, Jacob Smith has a big problem. His wagon is broke and he has to have it fixed today. I know hits Sunday."

The next three days, Johnson was moody. He spent most of the time in the blacksmith shop. When not repairing farm equipment or wagons, he made wrought iron items. He didn't have many silver dollars but was increasing his inventory of merchandise to sell and barter.

Before supper on Wednesday, his mother told him he should stop working and get ready to take Patty to church.

"Mom, I can't go tonight."

"Why not, Son?"

"I just don't feel like going to church tonight. Maybe I'll go Sunday."

Not even his mother knew a change was churning within her big son. He didn't have it all figured out yet, but it had something to do with his new thinking about life. Last Sunday in Sam's Cabin, a crazy thing happened to his thinking when his dad appeared. But before that, why did Jacob's wagon break on Sunday? Since then, the desire to make love with Patty before marriage was dampened. His softer, more considerate side, was surfacing to protect her from embarrassment or worse.

He went to Sam's Cabin after Thursday supper. It was like a light flashed before his eyes—a revelation—a roadmap—a decision. He would visit Carrie and Jane before marriage. He didn't sleep well until some time in the wee hours, when his plan changed.

Friday morning, the ninth of June, Johnson bid good-bye to his family. He was going to Clifton Forge,

Virginia to see a friend before getting serious about marriage. His mother grasped his hand and said, "Patty will make you a good wife. May the Lord be with you, Son, and return you safe to us."

About the same time Sunday afternoon, when Johnson was kissing Patty in Sam's Cabin, Oliver Cochran was kissing Carrie in her cabin. It was his first visit after returning from the war. His arm was bandaged but didn't hinder his first kiss with Carrie. After he left she thought and thought and guessed they would marry. They needed to discuss some details before a wedding date. She needed to tell him something. Her heart didn't want to do this, but practical sometimes prevails over love. Oliver had not acknowledged Jane during his hour visit. He didn't offer to help with any type of chore. When he was gone, her thoughts were that she would have rather kissed the porch post where Johnson once had his hand.

CHAPTER 15

"I remembered you like blue."

Hi Bill."

"Well, Johnson Perry it's good to see you again. What brings you to Lewisburg? I thought you . . . well Carl said you . . . but you look all in one piece."

"Carl was right—see, I made me a new leg and foot."

"Well, I say. That looks good, and you walk regular."

Twenty minutes later, Johnson had traded some of his wrought iron items for some of Bill's general store items.

The remaining trip to see Carrie and Jane zipped by like a breeze. The weather was great, and Johnson's spirits soared higher with each mile. He had calculated three and one-half days. His horse, Ginger, was ten years plus but a good steed. Midafternoon on a Monday, June 12, 1865, Johnson halted Ginger twenty yards from Carrie's cabin. He got out of the wagon and began walking toward the cabin. He was wearing a new, lightweight jacket with a western flair and a white Stetson hat. He saw no one until ten yards from the front porch—then a small girl with light brown hair, who couldn't have weighed more than a hundred pounds, shouted.

"Stop right there, Mister."

Johnson stopped and closed his eyes. He again remembered when he first heard such a command. He would never forget the character in her voice that cold, snowy night. The spirit and courage portrayed in those few words were the foundation of his love for Carrie. She had a rifle leveled on him, and her arms were still strong, because, he noted, the rifle was steady.

Johnson stopped. "I have a package for Jane Butler. Is she home?"

"Listen Mister, I don't have time for no carpetbagger. You best get your fancy dressed ass back in that rig and ride fast back up north."

She delivered the similar convincing message two and a half months ago but without the ass part.

"But I have this package . . . "

Johnson stopped as she stepped from the doorway onto the porch. With more grit and resolution, the five-foot-two gal barked another warning.

"I don't miss at this range."

Johnson turned and walked ten feet away from her before turning to face the rifle. He slowly removed his hat.

"I have two packages—one is for Jane and the other is Earl's underwear. The rifle was quickly lowered and Carrie ran in the cabin. Johnson stood in the doorway watching her cry facedown on the bed. Jane was in her playpen. She smiled and jabbered something when he picked her up.

Carrie refused to let Johnson see her until she had washed her face. He couldn't see why that would matter—he had seen her crying many times with her face wet and red with joy.

"Okay, Jane and I will take a buggy ride. You have ten minutes." He didn't intend to be bossy, but she had once given him orders.

Carrie put on her best dress and fixed her hair to receive a special guest—who she almost killed. She also started the coffee to heat. Gaiety showed in her smiles and bearing. "Johnson Perry, let me look at you. Your . . . your leg. Did you get a new one? How could that happen?"

"Yes, I have a new one. See, I made it."

"You did that?"

"Yep, me and my two hands in Dad's blacksmith shop."

"Gee, I didn't know you could do something like that. You walk right regular. Besides from your new leg and foot, you haven't changed, except you're more handsome."

"Must be my mamma's cooking."

Carrie didn't respond. Her happy mien changed to confusion. She just looked at him, trying to understand why his mother was cooking for him and not Sally Lou.

Johnson had been cheery and buoyant since arriving and was about to continue. "My, my, Carrie, you look great. Have you been all right?"

She answered with a barely audible, "Yes."

"Hey, I really do have a package. I'll go get it."

Carrie took advantage of his absence to think of a reason why he came. Something was different. He was more aggressive and more in command. Johnson bounced back in the cabin with a small package.

"Here Carrie, you open it."

"Johnson, you didn't have to do this. Oh! Look Jane, it's a little cap and your favorite color. Here baby, Johnsey brought it for you."

"I think she likes her new cap. She can wear it to church Sunday."

"Johnson, we don't go to church."

"Maybe it's time to start."

Carrie didn't answer him. Only a few ticks passed before Johnson happily announced he had a present for the lady of the cabin.

"No, no, I don't need anything."

"You mean you don't need *anything*?"

He didn't give her a chance to answer.

"You don't know it, but you need this present. You just stay put."

On the porch, Johnson began singing "Carry me back to old Virginy." After those six words, he continued singing accompanied by a guitar. He walked in the cabin singing and playing.

"Well, do you like your new guitar?" Again, he didn't wait for an answer. "Well, do you like it?"

"I can't play that thing."

"I know. I'm going to teach you."

"No, I can't play it." She was frustrated—something was wrong with the way he was acting.

"See, I have a book that shows you step by step."

Johnson looked at her beautiful face contorted with a bewildered expression. He had to divert his stare before her brown eyes impelled him to throw down the guitar and scoop her into his arms.

"Okay, okay, I'll put it on the table. I know you can learn. I've heard you sing, and I know a good singer when I hear one."

Johnson had to hurry on and stay in control. "You say you've been okay? How 'bout your garden?"

Not looking at him, she delivered an answer without much enthusiasm, "I have a small one."

Carrie had to know about Sally Lou soon or she would die. Again without ardor, she said, "Here's some coffee and two stale cookies. You will have to dunk them."

She wasn't looking at him when she asked, "John... Johnson . . . are you . . . are you marr . . . married to—"

He didn't let her finish. She received a robust answer.

"Glad you asked Carrie. I'm getting married this coming Saturday. How 'bout you—are you married?"

Carrie was nervous and overcome with grief because he was getting married. He never left her mind the past two and half months. She didn't really expect him back but still had hope that he would return and stay with her. All hope was now gone.

"He's getting married Saturday to his Sally Lou." Disgust and disappointment were boiling in her broken heart, but she was trying not to hate him. She curled her lip into a smirk and answered him.

"If I was married, wouldn't I have a husband with me? No! I'm not married.

With a less dynamic delivery, Johnson asked, "You're not married?"

"No." She was too embarrassed to tell him she and Oliver could also be married soon.

He quickly reverted to his vigorous manner of speaking. "That reminds me. I have another present for you. Come on the porch with me."

The first time these two met, Carrie gave all orders and commands. Johnson was still in charge right now.

He slowly walked back to the porch from the buggy and handed her a rather large, wrapped, flat box. Softly, he asked her to open her present.

She was startled with the contents. "Oh Johnson!"

"I remembered you like blue."

"But why?"

"It's a wedding dress. I figured you would be needin' one since soldiers are coming back home and . . . "

Both were silent. Finally, Carrie whispered with her head down, "So your life is working out like you and Sally Lou planned it?"

He answered in mellow but somber words, as he also lowered his head. "Carrie, Sally Lou got sick before I got back home. It was so hurtful. I figured out stopping here didn't matter because she . . . she . . . I . . . I didn't get to see her."

If Carrie was happy or sad, she didn't show it. She didn't react in any visible way—just stood motionless. Johnson went on to say that her sister, Patty, helped him understand what happened.

"I have been seeing Patty, who is sixteen. You know that sixteen is old enough to marry."

Carrie now reacted by going into the cabin. She left the dress in the rocking chair.

Johnson called for her to come back outside because he had something important to say. His little prank was turning out not to be so funny. When she didn't come out, he called again. After a few seconds, she told him that she was not going to watch him leave again.

"I'm not leaving. I'm coming in."

"No! Just leave. Why did you come back?"

She was standing by the fireplace with a disheveled expression revealing disappointment because Sally Lou's sister, Patty, was going to get *her* man. She was too angry to cry. Her frustration compounded when Oliver Cochran flashed in her mind and she thought, "Why is this happening to me?"

The once nonstop gal with a positive attitude now stood stooped, not wanting to hear anything else from the man who gave her the best days of her life. The one who had planted in her heart the hope of many happy tomorrows.

Johnson looked at the girl who taught him about love, who gave him an expectancy to live with the epitome of commitment and devotion. The girl with clinging arms and legs, who had lifted him higher than an eagle, consecrating the gift of love God gave man and woman. This girl of impressive courage and resolution stood slumped in spirit and stature. Her day had begun after a lonely, fitful night dreaming about Oliver Cochran. Jane was fussy all morning, and Johnson was adding salt to her wound of loneliness and disappointment.

The plan change he conceived just before leaving Falling Springs, was expressed in humble, sincere words.

"Carrie, I'm not going to marry Patty Foster. I come down here to say I want to marry you, but you don't seem to want me. The dress was for our wedding this Saturday. See, I have a ring."

Carrie stood stone-still with Jane in her arms. Her expression was frozen in a far away stare, as if trying to decipher the unexpected words spoken by the man she truly loved. Her short life had been a roller-coaster ride of highs and lows. The week with Johnson had been higher and sweeter than any dream she had ever imagined, and now the expectation from his proposal. . . Carrie never finished her thought—she fell across the rocking chair arms. By an instinctive reflex, she managed to prevent Jane from being totally crushed before Johnson rushed in and took the baby from her arms. He put Jane in her playpen and then gathered a limp Carrie in his arms. The strong-willed, competent gal who changed Johnson's life plan had fainted.

He took her to the bed and tenderly lowered her down. After a splash of water, she asked if she was in Heaven. Her quiescent expression before fainting had mutated into the countenance of an angel with tears streaming down her happy face. Johnson saw the change. He saw a transformation as miraculous as changing water into wine. A wine aged from her birth, with world-class endearments waiting to be a bouquet for him on this sunny afternoon. The ebullient young man of a few minutes ago was beyond being enthusiastic and excited.

"Carrie, I love you, I love you and I love you. Are you as happy as me?"

She stopped him with her hand on his mouth. "If only I could show you. Oh, Johnson, I *will* show you! I will! You and me will be happy for as long as I live."

He saw a rapturous glow on Carrie's angel face before he pounced on her—landing with such an impact that the bed collapsed to the floor. They laughed so hard that it was minutes before they could kiss.

Arm in arm, they walked around the yard and garden. Plans were discussed for another room after Johnson learned he would be a father in December. Of course there was shouting and hugging before the discussion - also some embracing which was different from the good news hugging.

Johnson milked the cows while Carrie prepared a special supper, including fried chicken and his favorite dessert—blackberry cake.

After Johnson declared he couldn't eat another bite, he cared for Jane until it was time for a buggy ride. Carrie had to tell Flossy and Granger the good news. There was not much talking during the ride back to the cabin. Carrie was tense, her mind sensitive, and body tingling.

The ten weeks Johnson was gone seemed longer than the hundred weeks she was alone before he knocked on her door. Without warning, her thoughts surfaced.

"You going to leave me again?"

"Yes, when I die."

"Can't you stay longer?"

"I'll work on it."

The sky was getting darker by the minute as they rode home. Ginger just made it in the barn before the rain. A warm breeze and gentle rain enhanced their desire for each other way before bedtime. Jane wasn't sleepy. The fire had to be banked, but embers restlessly loitered in two anxious hearts.

Once in the repaired bed, Carrie placed her left leg between Johnson's legs and her head on his chest. They immediately went to sleep—just kidding.

Later they were soundly asleep, but according to their old schedule, they were awake in the wee hours. They sat on the front porch wrapped in a sheet—Johnson in the rocking chair with Carrie on his lap. The sound of light rain softly falling on the metal roof was so soothing that Carrie quietly cried tears of exultation. Her partner couldn't stop thinking about the prize in his arms. Just before her heart burst from admiration for him, she whispered.

"Johnson my love, I have never been more happy than at this minute. Listening to the rain on the metal roof and being in your arms is about all the happiness my heart can stand. I have everything I need. I have my cabin my and farm with animals and a garden for food. I have Jane and your little one coming in December. But best of all, I have you. Oh Johnson, I have everything to make me the happiest girl in Virginia—No!—in the world."

"I know the feeling. I've been thinking about why I'm so lucky to have you."

"Well, I'm here for you to have."

Embracing incited caressing, while the rain would increase in intensity and then would be gentle again. It sounded like an opus that angels might have composed. Two lovers began trembling, which changed to giggling as they tried to get positioned in the rocking chair so Carrie could face Johnson.

The warm night air was filled with a summer rain symphony, blending with the sounds of a happy, reunited couple making love in a rocking chair.

EPILOGUE

The day after Johnson returned to Carrie, she made a dreaded trip to the store. This time she would not have Jane with her. Mr. Cochran acknowledged her as she stepped out of the buggy. He was distraught and immediately told her Oliver was in a coma. His wounded arm became infected, and he would not consent to amputation. She was sorry for Mr. Cochran but glad that she didn't have to tell Oliver about Johnson. She traded her butter and eggs for new shoes.

Saturday was a perfect day for a noon wedding. At 2 p.m., the newlyweds were . . . nope, not in bed . . . they were at Flossy and Granger's for a wedding dinner. Carrie's first ever invitation to a meal. When in Wytheville, she had eaten at her relatives', but this would be the first meal she didn't prepare or help prepare in some way.

It wasn't too long before responsibilities of married life hindered their fun time. Johnson had no blacksmith shop to make items to sell and barter. He worked odd jobs and would often return home late and tired. The new room had not been added when winter arrived. They did have plenty of food and cherished the presence of each other, always striving to give more than received. Cash flow was next to nil, and winter winds were blowing.

The day of the first snow, a letter arrived from Lillie. Mr. Perry asked Johnson to come home with his family. Lillie wrote, "Mamma is bad sick and wants to see her big son." Johnson, Carrie, and Jane made a hurried trip to Falling Springs, West Virginia. When back in Virginia, Carrie sold her farm to Flossie and Granger's son. The young Perry family returned to West Virginia on Christmas Eve 1865, to live in his parent's house. It was a joyous homecoming. Adding to the happiness, Andrew II was born just before midnight. Mrs. Lola Mae Perry died on the coldest day in February 1866. Johnson's father lived seven more years.

Robert, Johnson's younger brother, graduated from William and Mary College. He became a college professor living in Williamsburg, Virginia. He never married.

Lillie and Rachel married and settled on parts of the five hundred-acre farm that was willed to Johnson. Before Andrew Lee senior died, he requested that the farm always remain in Perry ownership. Johnson and Carrie had eight children, plus Jane. All eight children raised families while living on their part of Grandfather's farm. Jane married when fourteen and moved from Virginia to Independence, Missouri. A year later, she settled in Oregon's Williamette Valley via the Oregon Trail.

Patty Foster married Montgomery McMellon, a young doctor from Lewisburg, West Virginia. She stopped at Johnson's blacksmith shop one afternoon, five years after he returned to the farm. They briefly talked about their children before she asked to operate the bellows. She frankly told him her happiest days were with him, and she had thought about him often. He wiped tears while confessing he had also thought about her, but a higher power made the final decision to marry Carrie. He told her he and Carrie gave their hearts to Jesus four years ago. This prompted him to tell her that he had forgiven Sally Lou for not waiting. He told her if Jesus could forgive him for all he had done, including evil and lustful thoughts, then he was beholden to forgive Sally Lou. Tears filled Patty's eyes as she thanked him for forgiving her sister.

Patty had changed from the teasing and exciting gal he remembered. She looked more weary than happy. She was still beautiful, but her delightful spirit was gone. She wasn't the same girl he once planned to marry.

Wisps of sulfurous smoke encompassed them in an eerie quietness as scenes of another time circulated in their minds. Patty asked if he and Carrie were happy. His reply was a quick yes. Tears escaped from her brown eyes as she looked at the man who she would have married five years ago. She whispered that she would always love him and left before he could comment.

He had only seen her two other times in Lewisburg (with no talking) since the Sunday afternoon in Sam's Cabin. Johnson would not see Patty again after their tearful time in the blacksmith shop. She died having her fourth child. She was twenty-four years young.

Carrie did learn to play the guitar and became a local star. She wrote many songs, and she and Johnson performed within a three county area. Her most requested song was the first one she wrote—"I Can't Forget You." She changed the line—"While you're with your Sally Lou" to "While you're with your some one new." Young and old loved Carrie and Johnson. It was mostly her confident manner and talent that made them so well liked in their little part of Virginia. As their children and grandchildren matured, some joined the pickin' and grinnin' pair.

She didn't see Flossie and Granger again after leaving Clifton Forge, nor did she see any relative from Wytheville, except a niece who stopped on her way to Washington, D.C.

Years ticked away until it was a new century, and Johnson and Carrie had been married over thirty-four years. They were blessed with good children and grandchildren. Happy times had returned to their community. In 1913, the Falling Springs post office was renamed to Renick.

When the United States entered World War I, Andrew Lee III shouldered the impetus of his grandfather, who had marched off to war fifty-three years before. Andrew Lee III did not return back home from France.

Until the end of Carrie and Johnson's happy and contented life, they treasured their time together on the front porch. They were sitting there during a gentle summer rain on July 18, 1935. It was her eighty-ninth birthday. Their large family had been gone two hours. She and Johnson were reminiscing as they had oft before. They mentioned their first meeting, and as before, he would say he would have been mistaken for a Yankee and shot if he had had one more blue patch on his uniform. As always, she would say she didn't shoot because the Lord wanted them to have many happy years together.

She then smiled as a recording angel made an entry. Carrie Ann Perry's ticket was validated for a *one-way* flight to Heaven. Johnson joined her four months later.

THE END

ABOUT THE AUTHOR

Harry Beckett is a retired Engineer living in Barboursville, WV with his wife, Betty. Harry dreamed of writing a novel during his career of technical writing and his dream came true in 2002 when his first book was published. This book is his third with more planned during his retirement.

Music to Sally Lou's song is available by contacting the author by email.
tallskylark@juno.com